I Am Yours

Slave to Love, Volume 1

Alana Dyer

Published by Alana Dyer, 2023.

Table of Contents

Dedication

This novel is dedicated to all the people who have been struggling to free themselves and live their life to the fullest. To those battling their demons each and everyday and trying escape a reality they do not want.
Know that you are strong and the life you want is coming, just keep fighting!

Prologue

The nightlife is alive as the grand opening party continues. Risqué, the newest nightclub in town, is celebrating its first and rather successful opening, with men and women enjoying stolen moments in dark corners or pressed against each other, swaying to the sensual music. Two men sit together in a corner booth away from the low lighting, blending into the shadows. Although they are clearly outsiders to the party-goers, their attire is dark and non-descript, and dark shades cover their eyes. Their job tonight is to scope out new merchandise for their boss.

As traffickers for the largest slave shop, these men are tasked with finding women the rich find desirable, as the women will become slaves intended to please their masters in any way the men desire. Ready to call it a night, the two men get up, intending to go to a new spot, when they spot them. Three teenage-to-early-twenties girls enter the room, close to the table where the men were sitting just moments ago.

One of the girls has long hair that sparkles like a prism even in the dim light. Her locks sway as her body moves to the music, causing much of her hair to shift in colour. With one glance, the men knew she had a rare mutation only few people have after the Great War devastated Canada, the United States of America and the rest of the world two hundred years ago. The country of Symphrain was formed from part of Canada and the United States of America. To them, all this just means that the girl's shimmery hair is an all-natural rarity that allows her to fetch a high price.

The second girl has a short, aqua pixie cut and is wearing a cat ear headband that looks like it would shift out of place whenever she danced. She also has another rare hair type, making her another woman many men would fight over to claim as their own.

The final girl has hair as red as blood, vastly different from the traditional redhead seen in those of Old Scottish and Old Irish descent. Her hair is long and straight, not a curl in sight as she sways to the music. The two men could almost taste the profits to be had just by looking at these girls. They sported a slim, athletic figure of at least five-foot-three-inches, with full breasts that many women would resort to surgery for. Each has a tiny waist that can easily be held with one arm and an ass that just demands to be spanked. The men knew they'd hit the jackpot.

With the thought of a big payday in mind, the men go about luring each woman away, promising a night of dancing and getting each of them alone. They scouted out the back exit hours before, where they now bring the girls before drugging them, one at a time. Finally, with their three newly acquired merchandise secured in the back of the discreet black van, the men make their way to the Pet Shop with a grin on their faces. Tonight was a good haul for them.

༄

The shop owner smiles down at the new merchandise being carried into the shop. His men had done well with tonight's hunt and would be getting a good payout for the slaves they brought. The last van pulls in a good thirty minutes late for delivery, but as the two exit their vehicle to open up the back of the van, the punishment the shop owner was ready to order out pauses at the tip of his tongue. He already has two buyers ready for the aqua-haired girl; she will fetch a good price from a local man who is all too ready to gift his successful son. The second girl's blood-red hair is also eye-catching, and another buyer who has been looking for such a pet comes to mind. But the last girl is definitely a prize. She would make the perfect pleasure slave for a male.

Ordering the workers to deliver these girls into a holding room and his assistant, who has been waiting for news of specific pets, to make a call to the two gentlemen, the shop owner personally oversees the transfer of the prismatic-haired girl. With a flawless body and creamy white, fair skin, this girl will fetch a hefty price and make a well-earned profit for his pet business.

The maids take the unconscious girl into an exam room, stripping the girl naked and scrubbing her body clean. With her body ready, the shop owner motions for the Doctor to come in to do his examination. Her fingerprint is scanned, and her identity is revealed as eighteen-year-old Lyra Roselette, a perfect name and age for a pleasure pet. The Doctor continues his examination, testing each body part, making sure everything functions, and finally, coming to the last part of his assessment, checking to see if she is still pure. A pure pet will fetch the highest price possible as "Special Pets" bring more prestige to the Shop owner and their shop.

"You're in luck; this one here is a virgin!" The Doctor exclaims. The shopkeeper is thrilled and instructs which enhancement serums will be injected into her: one to stimulate her sex drive with just the slightest provocative touch, one to have her produce breast milk as many have demanded it in a pleasure pet, and one to make her soaking wet and craving for her tight virgin pussy to be fucked like the wanton whore she will be in the end.

After an hour of waiting for the completion of each injection, the Shop owner caresses her naked flesh, making sure the serums have worked their way through her system. Hearing the girl lustfully moan in her sleep, he wraps his lips around her right nipple, giving it a slight bite before he suckles, the warm taste of breast milk flowing into his mouth. His finger runs along the opening of her pussy, feeling the dampness of her juices flow out as she moans again, her hips moving on their own against the tips of his fingers. She is ready.

Signalling the maids to clean the girl and ready her for tomorrow, the Shop owner heads into a private room to deal with his own sexual frustrations using his own pet. As much as he would love to take Lyra as his own, he would rather have the money.

His mind wanders to the new merchandise as his cock rams in and out of his own pet, her moans and cries of pleasure fueling his imagination. Just what would Lyra sound like with a cock being rammed into her full force?

With his own fantasies being played out for an hour, the thought of using money to enhance one of his girls into a similar state as Lyra, the Shop Owner finishes, his hot seed filling the battered and spent slave under him. Coming out of the room now relieved, a maid informs him of the placement of his new merchandise, a gilded white-gold cage in the center of the shop. Taking a quick look inside, the Shop owner grins with the new display.

The new merchandise is wearing a white, lacy push-up bra as her shirt and a sheer skirt revealing the outline of her matching lacy thong. Her body lies elegantly on the swinging bed, a perfect specimen that will be the best sale of his career. The Shop owner adds the final touch of placing her information on the display screen in front of the door. Now all he has to do is wait for a wealthy buyer.

Chapter 1

I groan when the pounding headache caused by the lights turning on wakes me from my slumber. Burying my head under the cool pillow to block the lights from my face, I snuggle into the soft, warm bed and take a deep breath before sighing. But something felt off.

Last night my friends and I went out to party. I remember drinking and dancing, but after that, my mind is a complete blank. It must have been a good night because I can't remember much, but I wondered how I managed to get home safely. The feeling of something not being right returns to me when I hear the sounds of people moving about and multiple hushed voices. I live alone in my own apartment while attending school, so no one else should be home except me.

Deciding to investigate, I slowly push my sore body into a sitting position and open my eyes, even though my pounding head demands me not to do otherwise. Shock fills me with the view of about a hundred people milling about the room before me, filled with cages. Each cage is filled with a scantily clad human being, with the females wearing a matching bra and thong set and the males in just a thong themselves. They left nothing to the imagination with how each one looked.

Looking around, I realize I am placed in an elegant bird cage meant to fit a human and sitting on a swinging bed. I couldn't help but shiver with slight fear while I took in my situation. I, too, am also scantily dressed in a white, lacy push-up bra that barely contained my breasts and a thong with some form of sheer material as a long trailing skirt on top. The skirt has an opening at the front, revealing everything. I felt naked.

"You look lost, Darling." A voice behind me startles me from my questioning thoughts, making me turn around to see a woman wearing a maid uniform entering from a small door that blends seamlessly into the cage. I watch as she skilfully carries a tray with a silver dome to an ornate table, placing it down gently.

"I am a bit lost, if we are being honest. Where am I?" I ask the maid as she begins setting about food on the table. The smell of pancakes, sausages and hashbrowns causes my stomach to growl in protest, needing the nutrients the meal will provide.

"You're in a pet shop, silly, L'esclave Adoré, to be exact. You're to be sold to a new Master or Mistress." The Maid responds to my question cheerily. Dread fills me with her answer as I take another quick look around the room. L'esclave Adoré is a shop every girl steers clear of, knowing the dangers held within. The name is written in the rare language of French, meaning "The Adorable Slave." The shop has been in Lotross for over one hundred years, being the most popular in this trade for the wealthiest of the wealthy. And now, with many well-dressed patrons milling about the room peering into cages and dragging young women, men and girls that look less than legal age, the reality of where I sit sinks into me. My thoughts sink deeper into trying to remember what happened the night before and if I walked away from Aime and Jaida before being captured.

The smell of food brings me out of my spiralling thoughts, hunger pains bringing me back to the reality of being stuck in a gilded cage for all to see. The maid finishes setting the table as another sharp pain of hunger dictates my next move. Food will be the first step to surviving. Standing quickly, the world tilts on its axis, and I instantly regret my decision. A wave of dizziness washes over me, and the headache I awoke with is now amplified by the lack of food and the sudden spinning of the room.

"Easy now, Miss Lyra. The drugs are still wearing off on you." The maid scurries to my side, supporting my weak body before the dizziness causes me to fall to the ground. I give her a questioning look when she mentions drugs, wondering what was injected into my system. The maid seems to take the hint and gives me a sly smile as she helps me sit in the chair at the ornate table.

"You've been injected with three main serums. One helps your body to be susceptible to pleasurable touch." She trails her fingers along the curve of my breasts, causing a low moan to exit my mouth as my eyes flutter close. Her hands trail down my body, tugging at the bra and freeing my breasts as one hand stays to tug on the swollen bud and the other continues lower.

"One serum makes your pussy so sensitive; it's begging to be fucked." Her free hand finds its way between my legs and past the thin barrier of the thong to dive into my soaking wet pussy. Another lust-filled moan escapes past my lips, attracting an audience to watch the show. Her fingers move in a slow rhythmic movement building up a pressure inside me that begged for more. I grind my hips into the three digits inside me as the maid stretches my pussy with both pain and pleasure. The maid trails kisses down my neck until her lips find the free nipple, nipping at the bud before she suckles.

The warm flow of liquid leaving my nipple informs me I am producing breast milk, but the thought is washed away in pleasure as I edge closer to release. My moans attract a larger crowd enjoying the show while I catch a few people grabbing at their own slaves and exiting the room. The maid switches her lips from the abused sensitive nipple to the other and begins to suckle, causing my body to shiver with wanton need.

Finally, her fingers twitch one last time inside me, bringing me over the brink while my body is wracked with an orgasm. The chair below me becomes wet and sticky from my cum while the three fingers that have worked their way inside me slide out. The maid pulls away from my breasts, giving me a smirk while licking her fingers clean of my juices.

"The third serum causes you to produce breast milk. It's in high demand right now for pleasure pets like you." She announces as she slowly walks away from the table and towards the door. I am left panting, wondering what the hell I have been put into as my thoughts reel with this new information. The maid exits the cage leaving me all alone, sitting on a chair with a puddle of my juices and a large breakfast before me. I know security in this shop will be top quality as many shop proprietors in the slave training business will refuse to lose any of their *merchandise*, so planning an escape will be impossible. All I can do is wait for an opportunity and pray that the person who purchases me is nice and takes pity on my situation. My freedom relies on my attitude toward the person who will be my master or mistress.

With a sigh, I decide that wallowing in sadness will get me nowhere. If I want freedom, I need to keep my wits about me, and that begins with removing the knockout drug that I had a feeling was used on me. This required nutrients, and I had a heaping pile of food before me that would do just that. Picking up the silverware, I begin to eat. My plans are to keep up my strength, stay vigilant, find a way to escape, and then work on finding my friends. If I was captured and placed into a slave shop, then there's a high possibility of the same thing happening to Aime and Jaida.

My eyes were vigilant while I ate, watching as more patrons enter and leave the store, some with a purchase of a new human pet and others empty-handed. Eventually, my fate will be revealed.

Chapter 2

Time passes slowly after breakfast for me, causing my restlessness to kick in. I was never one for sitting still for too long; I prefer moving about and doing something productive. When the Maid returns sometime after eating, she hands me a damp towel to clean myself as she clears away the dishes and the wet mess of the chair before leaving me once again alone and on display.

As time passed, the pet shop became almost empty, with a few stragglers looking at what I learned was discount merchandise—Pets bought from poor families or used by multiple masters. These men and women were generally older than the usual pets, or so I've heard from the salesmen who handle the transactions. I felt pity for these people, but they all held an indifferent look when patrons would ask to look and handle them. They were used to this environment.

After walking three laps around the cage, rearranging the bedspread on the swinging bed, and sizing up the other pets in the cages before me, the Maid returns with a tray in hand. She places a platter of fruits down in the center of the table and explains it's a snack to munch on just before leaving me alone again.

Another wave of customers enters the building, each more ostentatiously dressed than the other. I hated the rich and how they looked down on others of the common class. Men and women alike gawk at me through the bars, but none linger too long near the cage. I was a commodity to them, something they would love to touch but not own.

The first person who took a real interest in me appeared an hour after the snacks were presented to me. He is a short, balding fat man whose body waddles around the room, and all I could think of is how my poor body would be crushed if he bought me.

Standing in front of my cage, I watch as this fat man's Assistant reads information about me on a display screen while the fat man tries to wipe away the permanent sweat that glistens on his face. Every detail about me is read word-for-word by the Assistant, from my medical history to the schools I attended, to the drugs injected into me when I got here. The one tidbit of information that horrifies me is the fact that my virginity is listed as an *added bonus*. Hearing that causes the fat man to stare at me like a hungry predator who has just found his next meal.

Relief fills me when the Assistant reads out the price set to purchase me. I watch as the predatory gaze falls to one of sadness as the fat man lets out a dejected sigh and walks away from my cage. It seems like I am too expensive to purchase by that man, and I am okay with that. I could only imagine the horrible life I would live if left to the fat man's *care*.

I watch the two make their rounds around each cage until the fat man spots a girl cowering in the corner. She is about my age with dark skin and big brown eyes, definitely a descendant of the now-rare African American race. His Assistant vanishes for a moment before returning with a maid who unlocks the cage, places a collar around the girl's neck and hands a leash to the fat man. He all but drags the young girl out of her cage and grabs at every inch of her skin. I can see the terror on her face as she is whisked away, begging for someone to help her.

The shop patrons ignore this show, probably used to a slave being dragged away, as they continue to shop around. A well-dressed man makes an appearance by my cage with the Maid who has served me and begins to talk in hushed tones as his eyes scan the crowd. With how respectful the Maid is, I assume he is this Shop's owner and is here to keep an eye on me.

The words *valuable merchandise* are spoken a few times between the two before the Maid disappears and the Shop owner sends me a wink. I guess this treatment means that I am the star of the show. It's funny, I wanted my cakes and desserts to be the star, the masterpieces that people around the world flocked to. Now, I am stuck. I wonder what will happen to my scholarship position. Will another person gain entrance to the culinary school, or will I be able to escape and continue my training?

Deep in thought, I did not notice the Maid returning to my cage, her voice calling out to me to come and eat lunch. A salad with grilled chicken is placed on the elegant table, its aroma causing my stomach to grumble. Taking a seat, I decide that starving myself will not help my chances to escape. I need to keep my strength up.

I wanted to give a big "fuck you" to the ones running this shop and eat like a slob, but years of my mother teaching me to eat like a proper young lady have me taking my time. The Shop owner walks around the floor, his eyes scanning each patron as they look into the cages. Many have begun to empty out with each new sale, but I have a feeling they will be full once again come tomorrow morning.

Of course, my actions do not go unnoticed as the Shop owner looks at me, his eyes roaming my body and the lady-like etiquette I portray, approval clearly displayed for all to see. No one would let me free as a well-behaved slave, and I realized my mistake in how I ate as the Maid cleared away the dishes. The staring continued until a spectacle occurred in a large cage across the way from me, drawing the patrons into a large crowd.

"Ladies and Gentlemen, welcome to the weekly Breeding Exhibition." The Shop owner booms, a grin on his disgusting face.

"Today, we will be allowing anyone to come and enjoy themselves with our newest breeder after our male has had his taste of her." He continues, a bed being wheeled into the cage as he speaks.

Tied to each post, a girl around my age stares wide-eyed at everyone, her orbs flicking to me with fear so prominent I have to turn and look away. If sex slaves, commonly known as pleasure pets, were the most sought after in the slave trade, breeders were the most frowned upon. They are worse than the common prostitute as their lives are dictated by whether they can produce new merchandise or not. A scream of terror hushes the crowd, a shiver running down my spine.

"Please, don't do this!" Sobs follow the girl's plea, and the shaking of chains indicates a pathetic attempt at freeing herself. The room fills with excited anticipation of the impending breeding. The sound of another cage unlocking catches my attention, and I watch as a young male with copper-coloured hair is led out of his cage by a pair of guards and past my own, where he sends me a flirtatious wink.

I feel shudders of disgust wrack my body as his lecherous eyes roam over me. I watch his figure enter the cage where the poor girl is stripped of her clothes, leaving her body for all to see. The male slave wastes no time getting to the prey offered before him, brushing off the guards and rushing to the girl's body.

Cheers from the audience roar around the room, followed by more sobs from the poor Breeder, the sound of flesh pounding against each other as the male lets out pleasurable grunts, his lips descending onto the delicate skin of the slave. Her fate is now sealed.

"Shop owner, will you let us breed with the girl in the bird cage?" My blood runs cold with fear, and my eyes meet that of a lanky man with graying hair, his tongue flickering out to lick his lips as his eyes undress what little fabric I have on my body. For once, I am thankful to be in this cage away from this man.

"No, Lyra here is special. If you have the money, you can purchase this pure slave." The patron looks away in disappointment, shrugging his shoulders as I watch each of his steps lead him away towards the cage where the poor Breeder is being raped for all to enjoy. The rich are sick with their twisted entertainment. As selfish as this thought is, I am glad I was not deemed a Breeder.

"You should watch Miss Lyra, as your job will be to pleasure your new owner." I jump in fright at the Maid now standing behind me, the woman silent in her approach.

"I don't want to." I retort, intending to ignore the scene across from me.

"It's not a suggestion. The Shop owner told me to tell you to. Trust me when I say you will be better off watching." My eyes move from the Maid to the Shop owner, who looks at me expectantly. The fear returns, knowing that even though I am valuable in his eyes, I am nothing more than an item to be sold. If I did not listen, then I would face the consequences.

My gaze slowly moves away from the man who decides my fate in this shop, returning to the scene in the cage across from me. Tears stream down the girl's face, her eyes gazing out at the crowd as she pleads for help, but none will come. I watch in horror as the male slave plows into her, knowing that this poor girl must be in pain. The pleading in her eyes is replaced with a sad acceptance before she lays listless on the bed, the male slave having an easier time with his conquest as his hips slam against the poor girl.

Moaning from the male and the slick squelch of his cock slipping in and out of her causes a bubble of fear to well inside me. I now know why the Maid made sure I watched. If I am not a good slave, I will be sold back to become a Breeder, especially with how rare my hair colour is, as I finally notice the unnatural way the light is reflected off of the Breeder's dark pink hair.

I hear the sound of men cheering as the male slave finishes his business, the satisfied growl from the male slave, loud and clear for all to hear, and the fight in the Breeder is now gone. I watch as the male pulls out, his cock now limp and light reflecting off the blood and cum coating him. If I ever get a chance to be free, I will fight for the abolishment of slaves.

"Thank you all for spectating this event. As promised, a signup list has been created for those who wish to participate. Please leave your name and contact information in case the child produced is yours. You will be able to enjoy her to your heart's content for one hour each." As the Shop owner's voice rings out over the crowd, I turn my attention away from the Breeder, her bed being rolled away from the sales floor to only God knows where. Her day will be long, judging by the signup sheet of sleazy males ready to give in to their carnal urges and fuck that poor Breeder senseless. This place is hell for anyone trapped here to be sold or used for the pleasure of the rich.

The Maid informs me that I am now free to do what I wish before bowing and taking her leave. Considering that I am trapped inside this gilded cage, there is nowhere for me to go but the table and the swinging bed. I am exposed just like that Breeder was for all to see. I want to run, be free and never return to this godforsaken place ever again, but even I know that this is a pipe dream.

Sighing, I close my eyes and send a silent prayer to any god or deity watching from above that I am set free soon, that I will be far away from this hell, living a normal life once again.

"Hello little Songbird, care to sing a song?" I stiffen in my seat, my eyes opening to see a man I can only describe as having Adonis-like features leaning on the bars to my cage. His cold and aloof emerald eyes stare into my own, with his dark chestnut hair falling over his eyes.

All I can think now is *be careful what you wish for.*

Chapter 3

"What's the matter, Songbird? Did the tiger catch your tongue?" The man chuckles, his cold eyes continuing to stare into my own. His lips curl into a slight grin, the smile never reaching his eyes. At once, I felt like prey caught in the deathly stare of a predator. The room is silent, with no bustling of noise nor pleasure from the slaves as the onlookers wait to see what will happen next, like a scene in a play.

The man is studying me, as all customers do, but his eyes leave goosebumps on my skin in their wake. He is dressed in black jeans with a black belt, a navy dress shirt that barely conceals the massive muscles underneath, a worn-out leather jacket with a pair of designer sunglasses hanging out of the chest pocket, and a pair of black combat boots to finish the ensemble. Nothing screams special about this male other than the look of a stereotypical rich kid of the capitol. What has me on edge is how everyone around us has quieted down to stare at the young male as if he is some sort of celebrity or idol.

"Welcome, your Highness! Did you find a slave that interests you?" The Shop owner exclaims, breaking the tension in the room with a single phrase. Realization settles in with these words; Alekai Nightwood, the heir of Symphrain, stands before me. The two men quietly converse about what the prince came for, probably a slave to serve his every desire. If the Crown Prince is here, then that means some unfortunate girl will be taken away to the Palace, a place I feel could be deadly for a slave. I try to find a way to hide from view, even knowing that any attempt is futile.

"-and I would like to hear her sing. If I like her voice, I will pay three billion dollars for her." I clue into the conversation at hand just outside my cage, Prince Alekai motioning in my direction with a smirk on his face. Shock fills me at the price offered for my body. This Prince is willing to pay three times the amount for me if he likes my voice. Gasps sound around the room, and I have a feeling that not many slaves are sold for such a large sum. This transaction of me becoming Prince Alekai's property will be the largest yet for this pet shop.

"Oh, Lyra here will gladly sing for you, and if she refuses, there will be a punishment waiting for her." The Shop owner answers for me, with a warning look sent my way. I swallow hard as I think of the memories of being beaten by my drunkard of a father growing up. I hated pain, especially if that pain was caused by something I never did. It was all I knew as a child and was why I moved out as soon as I could afford culinary school.

"So, Little Songbird, care to sing the Anthem?" Prince Alekai asks, but his tone leaves no room to refuse. Refusing the Crown Prince meant punishment, or worse, death. The anthem is a song drilled into every citizen since the day they are born. It is to make us proud of our country that rose from the great World War Three that devastated the former countries of The United States of America and Canada, leaving half of each country habitable, the rest a wasteland. Anticipation of what my next move will be and whether I will defy the prince becomes the topic of the patrons in hushed tones. Taking a deep breath to settle my nerves, I close my eyes and picture that I am in my own room.

"Free to Be
Free to Roam
Oh Symphrain
we call our home
From the ashes, we will rise
Into the great, clear blue sky
Our hearts filled with love
That we cannot hide –"

I feel like a bird stuck in a cage, forced to perform at the whims of a man who holds power over my life and death at this very moment. To the masses around me, I am a Songbird here only to amuse him and other shop patrons. But I have no other choice other than to continue singing.

"A life of wonder
A life to roam
We forever will call Symphrain our home
From the deep blue sea
To the city's night

Our wings they glide
as we take flight
No longer lost
No longer we roam
For Symphrain is our forever home"

I hold the last note as the song comes to an end. All throughout my song, the room remained quiet, the audience captivated by the little Songbird in the gilded cage, captivated by me. Roars of applause and an encore cause me to open my eyes just in time to see Prince Alekai hand the Shop owner a suitcase, one I already know is filled with money that was promised before my performance. I was sold to a man rumoured to be cold-hearted and cruel, a man whose being can send shivers of fear to anyone who crosses his path.

I am now sold to the Crown Prince as his pleasure pet for him to do whatever he wishes to my being. Time passes in a blur with the Prince and the Shop owner disappearing; whispers among the patrons soon build to a conversation about how lucky Prince Alekai is to purchase me. Sympathetic glances from those in cages around me are sent my way, some probably already sending a prayer to me with their thoughts on my impending demise. Most slaves sold to royalty or nobility never make it out alive. The sound of the cage doors swinging open, the bars crashing against each other with a loud bang, alerts me to the presence of another person inside the prison I woke up in. Loud footsteps upon the metal floor make quick work where I sit frozen with an unknown fear. Turning to face the intruder in my cage, I come face to face with a tall male in a black suit, my face reflected in his mirrored sunglasses.

His build screams bodyguard, one not to mess with and one to fear if his charge is attacked in any way. Muscles bunch with each determined stride under his fitted suit as each step leads him closer to where I sit. My eyes search for a way to avoid this unknown man, not wanting his hands on me in any way. Seeing a clear view of the open door and a chance at freedom, hope ignites a flame of determination inside me.

All I have to do is run around this unknown man and fight my way out. Taking a deep breath to steady the nerves from the fear that fights against my determination to escape, I fling myself from the chair and rush to the cage door, making sure to keep as much distance from the unknown man as possible. Freedom is in reach as my mad rush confuses the man for a moment, the wide-open door to this gilded cage growing closer and fueling the flame of determination into a raging inferno inside me.

But then I feel the floor of the cage shaking as the man—now behind me—chases after me. If I can just make it outside the cage, I can lock the man inside and work on getting out of this shop. Pushing my body to its limits, I focus solely on exiting the cage and getting past the patrons of this shop. If I could make it to the street outside, I could blend into the crowd and get home. Then I feel them, strong hands grasping my upper bicep in a vice grip, pulling me back with fingers digging into my skin where I know I will bruise by tomorrow morning. The man begins to drag me none too gently out of the cage; my attempt at escape, in hindsight, was futile.

"Alex, have your men handle her with care, or your store will be arrested for damaging Royal Property!" A shout is heard, followed by another pair of hands pulling me away from the man, Prince Alekai's glare reflected in the other man's sunglasses.

"I'm so sorry, your Highness. I will punish him later." The Shop owner, who I learn is named Alex, says in a high-pitched, snivelling voice, probably looking to get into Prince Alekai's good graces in hopes of the Prince visiting the shop in the future. Silence and a dismissive hand are all the Shop owner receives as his cue to leave the Prince and me alone, fear overtaking me once more with this looming monarch standing before me.

"If I have to drag you out of the store and into the limousine, you will regret it." The threat is low, but the nods of approval from nearby patrons catch my attention. It seems like my life and death are held in this man's hands. With a nod of his head, Prince Alekai leads me away from the golden bird cage and towards the exit, his hand clutching my wrist in a grip that was not painful but strong enough to keep me restrained and thwart any attempt at running away.

My eyes continue to scan the room for any way to escape, or any way to gain sympathy and help. But everyone turns away to look at the many cages we pass by, one even holding children, which makes my heart break at the sight of them. This is the cruel world we live in.

With a sigh, I am pulled past another door, my eyes adjusting to the brighter room as the sounds of puppies barking and cats meowing for attention fill my ears. We were in the normal pet shop part of this store, where the concerns of human slaves and pets were unnoticed by those going through the mundane in hopes of having a furry little companion for their normal lives. After walking past many displays and supplies, the two of us reach the exit quickly, his grip on my wrist ever-present as we exit the store and onto the streets.

Standing on the sidewalk in the trendy part of Lotross, the wind leaves a chill on my barely covered skin, causing goosebumps to form as I shiver in the fall air. A gleaming silver limousine with the Royal crest on the doors waits for us on the curb. A man I assume to be the driver for Prince Alekai bows to us as he opens the door silently, his face holding a blank expression as if the world around us has no meaning to him. I can already tell he would be no help in my escape.

Taking the final steps towards the vehicle, Prince Alekai pushes me into the limousine without warning, leaving me sprawled on the plush leather seats. Before I could move away from the man who now owns me, the Prince slides in gracefully, taking hold of my wrist and pulling me onto his lap and against his solid body. One arm holds me in place, snaking around my waist and thwarting any attempt to move away. His free hand roams my body, causing the drugs coursing through my system to make my skin shiver with pleasure. A soft moan escapes my lips when a gentle kiss from the Prince is placed on my neck, a kiss that turns into a smirk.

"You are mine, Little Songbird. It's only a matter of time until I claim every inch of you."

Chapter 4

The purr of the engine brings my attention to the car moving forward, away from the pet store. Streets pass by, and the thoughts of escaping vanish. Instead, I am trapped with strong arms wrapped around me as Prince Alekai's lips roam from my neck down to my collar bone, the enhancement drugs causing my body to slowly heat up with this erotic action. A small moan escapes my lips when the Prince bites me gently, a chuckle being his response.

"I am not one for enhancement drugs, but I do enjoy the benefits they bring." he whispers into my ear, one of his hands freeing my breast from the skimpy top, the other moving to draw slow circles on my stomach. The Prince continues his ministrations, lips kissing any free skin while both his hands find their way to groping me, fingers pinching the hard buds that are my nipples.

"P-please stop," I stutter out in a whimper, squeezing my legs tight, trying to stop the ache from building.

"Sorry, Little Songbird, but if I stop, I won't be satisfied, and I'll end up doing more." Prince Alekai answers, his voice husky. Lips replace fingers as his mouth descends upon my breast, rolling the hard bud between his teeth and sending shocks of pleasure coursing through me. His free hand is pushed between my legs, where the tips of his fingers find the wet material that barely blocks my entrance from his exploration.

My mind is hazy with the pleasure his lips and hands bring, Prince Alekai changing from biting my hard nipple to sucking on it, the feeling of liquid flowing out as the milk produced is suckled and drank by him. Strong fingers tear away the material guarding my wet pussy before being pushed deep inside me, massaging my insides as a low sensual moan escapes me. All sense of time leaves me, the pleasure building inside with each stroke of these fingers, my juices seeping out.

My hips involuntarily grind against him, my mind focused on only the pleasure and relief I seek to the pressure that keeps building, as the sounds of my moans and Prince Alekai suckling from my breasts fill the limousine. The speed of the fingers inside me increases, causing me to cry out as my walls twitch and squeeze, relief of orgasm crashing down around my hazy mind.

Taking deep breaths, I finally break through the haze that consumed me to find myself laying on my back. Prince Alekai is above me, licking his fingers clean from my cum as he grinds into me, his pants the only thing separating his hard bulge from taking my virginity as the car comes to a stop.

"Guess I'll have to wait for tonight to take every inch of you." He chuckles with a grin on his face. I go to move, but the Prince is too fast as I find my hands pinned above me with his lips, still holding the tase of my cum and breast milk, claiming mine. His tongue invades my mouth while he continues to grind against me, the pressure building once again and turning my mind into a hazy mush. Still, I pray that something makes this stop as I want to find some way away from the man above me, my body feeling used and dirty from the way the Maid at the Pet Shop and Prince Alekai has touched me.

Then, as if answering my prayers, a knock on the window snaps the Prince away from me, bringing me some relief while I distance myself from him and rearrange the skimpy clothes to cover myself as best as possible. He chuckles at my movements, shaking his head at me as I glare back at Prince Alekai before the door is opened, and I am left alone to my thoughts as Prince Alekai leaves the limousine. I was kidnapped and turned into a slave—a sex slave. I was bought by the Prince of this nation. And if I stay here with no chance of escape, I will lose my virginity quickly to a man that only sees me as his property and nothing else. What I need to do now is escape, and soon.

"Miss Lyra?" I jump, hearing a light musical voice from outside the vehicle before a face greets me with a warm smile.

"Hello. His Highness would like for you to come with me and have you prepared for later tonight." Dread settles into me as I take in the appearance of the young woman before me. Her chestnut-coloured hair is pristinely pulled on top of her head and styled into a neat bun. Her gaze is warm as she smiles at me, the wind ruffling her black and white uniform that she pushes down to keep from riding up. What finally clues me into her position here in the palace is the apron tied around her waist. I had seen this familiar uniform many times in Aime's studio, with her father and her supplying the uniforms for the Royal Palace workers. She was one of the maids that worked here and, if I am correct, is assigned to Prince Alekai's wing.

"How do you know my name?" I ask wearily, refusing to move from my position in the limousine as the Maid and I stare at each other.

"The driver called ahead of time when the Prince purchased you. Everything you need is already assembled and waiting in the Prince's chambers where you will stay."

"How can that be when you don't know my size or-"

"We know everything about you, Miss Lyra, from the bra size you wear to your medical history." My face blanches at her statement, and I take a deep breath. My privacy is gone, and so is my life at this point. But the chance of escape still had hope simmering inside me.

"Now, if you will get out, I will take you to the Prince's room." Her words left no room for an argument. To this Maid, I was a pet, a person meant to comfort my owner. I am not a human being anymore in the eyes of the law and could be treated like a dog led on a leash. I did not want to be led away from the safety of the limousine just to be the Prince's plaything but I had no choice but to obey this Maid. Refusal would most likely lead to punishment.

With a sigh, I slide closer to the door watching the Maid back away to the side and allowing me to exit. The view before me as I stood, as I stretched my cramped muscles from being confined and played with by Prince Alekai, took my breath away. The Palace, a five-story white brick building with ivy growing along some crevices, looked like a place out of a fairytale. Around the palace were impeccable gardens with fountains full of crystal clear water.

Turning to look back at the limousine, I realize that other than the Maid and the Driver climbing back into the vehicle and myself, no one else is around. This sparks a tiny bit of hope as I take this chance to run, my body moving on its own down the elaborate driveway, hoping to find my freedom. But my escape is short-lived as guards appear out of nowhere, surrounding me with no room to maneuver around them.

"Miss Lyra, please understand that we cannot let you leave. You are the Prince's property, making you a royal pet. If you were to escape or be injured under our watch, we would be heavily punished." The Maid appears behind me, her face an emotionless mask as I turn to face her. At this moment, I realize that I am condemned to the fate of a pet. I have to give up any hope of escape now as the guards surrounding me would stop any movement I make by force. With no choice in my own life anymore and shoulders slumping in defeat, the guards take this as their cue to guide me back towards the Palace entrance, the Maid placing a hand on the small of my back, probably to grab me the moment I try to make another futile escape.

"Thank you, gentlemen, but I think I can handle the Prince's pet from here." Once inside the Palace entrance, the grand doors are shut, and I am left to stare at what will be my new home. Unfortunately for me, the Palace would be more like a prison for many years to come.

"Miss Lyra, I know you are not here on your own accord, and I am sorry, but orders are orders for me. I am Elisa, the maid responsible for ensuring you are safe and well-groomed. To the people working and living inside the Palace, I am your handler. But hopefully, you can count on me as a friend." I just nod at Elisa as she explains her role and what is expected of me as a pet, unable to enjoy the beauty of the Palace interior while she takes my arms and leads me up the grand staircase.

"As you know, the Prince has yet to choose a Princess consort. As such, the King recommended he get himself a companion from the pet store. It was a way to ensure that if the Prince owned the companion, then the Royal family would not have to deal with a scandal on their hands. This is why you are here." Elisa continues to talk endlessly, filling the quiet ascent with rules and regulations within the Palace: how a pet is supposed to act during Royal Balls and Formal Events, how a pet is required to dress, where a pet is allowed and forbidden. Rules will be the shackle to said prison. After climbing three floors, my legs were beginning to feel heavy, and I was happy when Elisa led me towards the right corridor instead of turning to climb the fourth set of stairs.

"Stand still." She orders me, and I comply. A gold chain is slipped around my neck, tight enough that I cannot pull it over my head to take it off but loose enough to slip two fingers between the chain and my neck. A single gold chain is attached to the main one with a charm dangling from it. I wasn't stupid and realized that the charm was the royal crest but altered with two wolves on either side of the crest. This was a collar to match the shackling rules and further my status as a pet.

"This is the Prince's crest, and this necklace is only removable with his thumbprint. You are free to roam the Palace grounds, and this chain not only keeps you from leaving without the Prince by your side but also lets others know who you belong to." Elisa pauses her speech as I absorb her information. I could explore the Palace without repercussions on my own but would be trapped inside without any escape. This collar is designed in a way it could not be tampered with and I had a feeling that there is more to it.

"You are allowed outside of the Palace with his Highness but understand that if you leave his side for more than a ten-meter radius, you will be injected with a drug that will render you weak and possibly immobile while the GPS tracker alerts someone to your position so that you can be collected." She continues before motioning me to follow her.

"This floor belongs to the Prince, and it is where you will live. You are to be in the bedroom by nine o'clock each night, but other than that, you are free to do as you please unless the Prince gives you an order." Lead to a massive double oak doorway, two Guards on either side open the entrance, revealing a large, brightly lit sitting room. A massive flat-screen television is mounted on the wall opposite the door above a stone fireplace, a fire already roaring and warming up the room. Plush black sofas look enticing, and the thought of sitting on them crosses my mind. The final touch to this room is a small kitchenette off the side with floor-to-ceiling windows letting in the sunlight.

Without a chance to explore the first room, Elisa takes my hand, pulling me with her towards another set of double doors opened and waiting for us to step through while the guards close the first set. This time I am greeted by the sight of a large bedroom, a king-size canopy bed with a red and gold covering and a mountain of plush pillows waiting for me. I swallow hard, knowing that this will soon be the bed I share with Prince Alekai. Again, the room has floor-to-ceiling glass windows with another wall full of built-in bookshelves split in half by a large tapestry with the same crest on my necklace and a few armchairs placed in front of the beautiful tapestry. This will be a perfect reading nook to relax with a good book full of natural light. If the foreshadowing of my impending virginity loss weren't dampening my mood, I would have been excited to have a room like this.

"There's more to this room, Miss Lyra." Elisa smiles, beckoning me to follow her, which, unfortunately, I have to no matter what. Leading me across the room towards another set of double doors, Elisa smiles mischievously at me, motioning me to take the lead.

"I think this might be your favourite part of the living quarters, Miss Lyra." Frowning at her secrecy, I cautiously step towards the doors, grasping each handle and pausing to say a silent prayer hoping for protection. Finally, with a push, the doors open, revealing a bright room. Once again, the windows are floor to ceiling, contributing to the bright space. But what is most shocking is that this is a large bathroom designed as a spa. Cream curtains are pulled back to allow the light to filter into the room, matching the cream walls that give the bathroom a warm and relaxing feel. A large shower sits in the far-right corner, made out of black marble with the glass sparkling as if translucent. One would have to look closely, or else they could walk into the glass walls. On the left side of the room sits a vanity with his and hers sink combination, the wall a mirror to allow one to get ready easily, and beside that is a shelf that holds every last form of bath product from bath salts to bubble baths and everything in between. The most magnificent piece though is the large black marble infinity bathtub that sits in the center of the room closest to the windows. Steam rises into the air as the water continues to flow, creating a surreal effect as the scent of roses and mint fills the air. I yearned to soak away the disgusting feeling of the Slave Market and the stress accumulated this morning, wanting nothing more to fade into the water and hopefully come up in my own home as if this was all a bad dream. But the cool chain around my neck reminds me this is reality.

"It's time for you to bathe Miss Lyra. After that, the prep team will be here to prep your body." Elisa states, leading me towards the infinity tub and helping me undress. She bids me goodbye, stating she would be back within two hours after the beauty specialists have helped me scrub the grime away and freshen me up, allowing me some form of privacy for a moment. I climb into the tub, realizing there is enough space for three people and sigh. I have a feeling the Prince would want to enjoy some quality time in here.

The hot, scented water does wonders in helping my muscles relax, my body feeling like it is melting away as I submerge myself underneath for a few seconds, letting my mind go blank while I slowly accept reality. This is my fate. No longer was I a culinary student studying to better my life. I was a pet, owned for my master's pleasure. I could either accept the role and the luxuries that come with it or die trying to escape. An idea pops into my mind, and I surface from the water, lean back against the tub and smile as I look out the window. I could accept the luxuries of my stay while looking for a way to escape. Why waste an opportunity of pampering, as I have a feeling I would be stuck here for a while until I can regain my freedom.

Sometime later, three ladies dressed in a light blue uniform stroll into the bathroom, each pushing some form of cart and readying the equipment quietly to the side. I watch curiously, wondering what their plans are as I realize these ladies are the prep team. Finally, two finish their current job and come toward me with friendly smiles.

"Hello, Miss Lyra. We are here to help you bathe and prep your body." The first one speaks. She is short, maybe five-foot-three inches, with curly red hair contained as best as it can be in a messy bun. Her tanned skin matches her curly red hair and bright green-friendly eyes beautifully, and I smile back at her.

"I won't be difficult since it's your job." I reply, giving them permission to do what they must do. The second lady sighs as if in relief, most likely worried I would throw a fit and make things difficult for them. But being from a damaged home and poverty, I understood their fears better than anyone else.

The second lady is a curvy woman with braided black hair and dark, almost chocolate-coloured skin. She is of rare African American descent and carries her heritage proudly, from what I can tell. The war really took a toll on the human population, and many cultures were lost. It is refreshing to see this woman working happily, and with her skin glowing beautifully in the sunlight, I just know I am in capable hands.

She turns and walks to the shelves, picking and choosing from the products, sometimes placing a container back in favour of another. When she returns to her partner's side, the two women get to work, helping me to scrub my body clean and being careful not to touch any sensitive spots that would cause a reaction due to the stupid drugs the Pet Store injected into me.

Their hands are gentle yet firm as they helped ease even more tension from my body. I felt like a princess in the moment, letting my body relax in their care as the grimy feeling from this morning washed away. Once declared fully clean by the ladies, the two help me out of the tub and help me dry off, both complimenting me on my hair and body, while the third woman fiddles with more equipment and prepares a massage bed where I am finally led to and asked to lie down.

"The next process may hurt Miss Lyra. Please bear with it for now." The redhead warns, giving me a sympathetic look before a table is rolled towards me, and the unmistakable smell of wax reaches my nose. I understand what is next as Aime loved getting her eyebrows waxed, and if the warning is true, I am not going to like the next phase. As if on cue, the ladies begin to spread wax onto every part of my body, apologizing along the way as I cry out in pain. Tears flow freely from my eyes as the experience is something I never thought would happen.

"We are almost done, Hun. The last part, unfortunately, will be the most painful." I just nod, asking for a moment to ready myself as they clean up the current mess and prepare for what I learned is a bikini wax, one that left me very sore. All hair was gone, except for my now perfectly sculpted eyebrows and soon-to-be styled and cut hair.

"Now is the best part, Miss Lyra. Just close your eyes and relax." The third woman says with a musical lilt to her voice. Before I know it, the ladies smooth warm oil onto the sore parts of my body where the wax has removed any hair. The massage slowly soothes my aches as the scented oils calm my mind. Before I know it, I find myself dozing off to sleep.

Chapter 5

My eyes slowly open to the quietness of the room, my body feeling well-rested, with the tense muscles from my usual stress-filled days gone. I felt light and agile. Sometime during the massage, I must have fallen asleep as I find myself now lying in the large bed, the duvet covering my now relaxed body. I feel warm and cozy, but reality crashes down when I move to get more comfortable and realize there is something attached to my feet.

Jolting awake, I fling the duvet off of me, taking note of the heels now carefully strapped onto each foot. I remember my body being naked under the prep team's care, but now I sat in the large bed in a flowing, almost sheer, dress and, after further inspection, a lacy white thong and push-up bra set. Someone must have dressed my unconscious body after the massage put me to sleep, and the thought of this causes goose bumps to form on my skin and shivers to slowly crawl down my spine. I prayed that the prep team was the one to dress and move me.

Deciding to stretch and explore what is my room for the rest of my life, I gingerly climb out of bed and carefully return the duvet back into position, leaving the bed as if no one had slept in it. That's when I noticed a slightly crumpled note on the bed that must have gotten mixed into the duvet when I threw it off of me. Reaching for the note, my eyes widen at the manicured hands in front of me, shocked at how beautiful and elegant my normally rough hands are. My nails are rounded at a comfortable length that allows me to still do everyday tasks, the colour a pearlescent white with black French tips. The only design is the Prince's crest on each ring finger, with a gem twinkling in the light just above the design. For once, I felt like a woman, not a child from the slums who fought her way out. Once done examining my nails, I reach again for the note and read the contents.

Lyra,

I noticed you asleep and dressed after the prep team
took care of you and decided to lay you in bed. Feel free
to explore the palace, as it is your new home, and I want
you to be comfortable.
Just remember your curfew.
Sincerely,
Alekai

I smile with this note, happy to know I have free reign to travel inside the Palace without an escort. Then, throwing the note onto the nightstand, I stride out of the room happily, ready to find my escape.

∞

I groan in frustration, finding myself facing another dead end with a portrait of some dead royal looking down on me as if mocking me for my directionally challenged brain. I felt lost and defeated in this maze-like Palace, finding many dead ends or servant quarters, but never an exit to the outside. Many servants see me but ignore my presence as if I am nothing but a ghost. Apparently, slaves and pets were nothing in their eyes other than something to prevent from leaving. No one asked if I needed help finding my way or asked if I was lost. I felt alone in the halls with no companion to talk to and no one to help me. With a sigh, I turn the way I came, coming to a stop at the four-way intersection in the halls. Straight leads me to the grand staircase where the rooms and studies are and the entrance to the Palace; behind me is a dead end. But left and right were unknown areas yet to be explored. And then my stomach growls, protesting the lack of food and reminding me the only thing I have eaten is the breakfast at the pet shop this morning.

As I decide which way to take, the smell of pastries baking catches my attention from the right hall, causing my stomach to rumble once again. With a new goal in mind of getting food, I walk down the hall on the right, following the smell that fills each crevice with its mouth-watering aroma. More doors lead to unknown rooms while servants stare and whisper as I pass by, reminding me that I am alone here in this beautiful prison. I decide to ignore them and continue on this quest to fill my grumbling stomach as soon as possible. With each step, the smell of Danishes, rolls and my favourite, croissants, became stronger upon arriving at the entrance to a glorious kitchen. The room is brightly lit with more floor-to-ceiling windows on the east side that looks out into a garden, one I assume is filled with vegetables and fruit, an easy supply of fresh produce for the Palace. The south side of the room is filled with shelving, a door to what I assume is an exceptionally large pantry, and the unmistakable doors to a walk-in fridge. Ovens and stovetops line the north side of the room, the smell of pastries coming from them making my stomach growl again in protest of being empty.

"We have extras, darling, if you're hungry." A friendly voice steers me from gawking at the kitchen, my hands itching to get in there and cook alongside the staff. I turn towards a woman in her mid-thirties, her curly blonde hair piled on top of her head in a messy bun as she carries a hot tray full of strawberry vanishes by its smell.

"Please, I am starving," I answer graciously, walking towards a picnic bench that this friendly woman motions me towards. I smile when she sets the tray down and accepts a plate from another staff member, where she promptly plates two Danishes and hands the plate to me.

"Thank you!" I quickly mutter, taking a bite of the delicious treat, smiling as the woman waltz around the kitchen with a small basket, filling it with goodies from cookies to pastries and everything in between, before coming to a stop at the bench and taking a seat, pushing the basket towards me.

"You look like you are enjoying those," she chuckles, motioning to my nearly empty plate, causing me to blush.

"Yeah, it's the second thing I have eaten today since early morning," I answer, blushing in embarrassment. The woman laughs some more, giving another staff member an order to bring me a bowl of soup that is promptly placed in front of me with a fresh-baked roll that I promptly dig into and enjoy.

"I'm Ali, by the way. Don't mind my bluntness, but you must be the Prince's new Pet the Palace maids are gossiping about." I groan at her words, leaning against the wall and sighing as I stir the soup, my appetite slowly dissipating at the mention of the unhelpful maids and my situation.

"I'm Lyra, and yes, I am his pet." I sigh out sadly, pushing the half-empty bowl away and looking wistfully at the kitchen staff working away with baking and prepping food for the Palace.

"In all honesty, I would rather be here slaving away at the stove making delicious food than dressed up like a fashion doll for someone to play with." My eyes tear up, feeling the unfairness of the situation and how I would never graduate from college. How I will be stuck here, unable to do anything but be used and abused by a pampered prince with no sense of humanity.

"You cook?" Her question causes me to smile and nod, turning to face this potential friend.

"I am a culinary student at the college downtown. This was supposed to be my first year, and I would enter an apprenticeship when the school year ended for a year before going back for my last year." I answer honestly, looking back towards the kitchen staff, itching to cover my hands in flour and bake a few loaves of bread.

"I'm sorry, sweetie." Ali is up and by my side, giving me a very needed and comforting hug.

"It's not your fault." I smile at the warmth, hugging this woman back and letting myself shed a few tears into her apron that smelt like fresh bread and cookies. A comfort that eased the sadness of my lost future.

"I know it isn't, but someone needs to apologize for this injustice to you, hun. If it makes you feel any better, you are welcome to come to my kitchen and cook. I am the head chef here and could always use a new pair of hands, especially one who clearly has an interest in the culinary arts." I smile, feeling a glimmer of hope for once as Ali gives me an opportunity I did not expect. Maybe this could be a way to get information and escape from Prince Alekai and the Palace.

"That would be amazing, Ali, thank you!" I take her hand, watching her wince and quickly let go, remembering the nails I now have.

"You're welcome, and next time you're here, I should have a pair of gloves because damn girl, those nails are sharp." She cracks a joke, pointing to my perfectly manicured hands. Hands I will have to get used to eventually. The rest of the time is spent talking with Ali and the staff. The staff consisted of ten women and five men, each accepting me for who I am as a person and not my status as a pet. Due to my outfit and appearance, I couldn't help with the cooking, but I did enjoy talking to everyone. I felt like I belonged in this part of the Palace, that my role as a pet was forgotten as I laugh and relax with everyone. Then the clock chimed, signalling the time as eight o'clock at night. I had lost track of time with everyone, and dread filled me.

"Lyra, you okay? You look like you've seen a ghost!" Max, a cook, states with worry. I stand quickly, rushing to my basket of goodies on the picnic table and heading to the door.

"I have to return to the Prince's bedroom before nine. Elisa told me I would be punished if I am late, and I don't think I could handle that right now." I answer honestly, fear taking hold. The scene of the female slave being raped and bred like cattle plays in my mind, and I begin to hyperventilate as anxiety takes hold. "Lyra breathe, honey, breathe!" Ali is by my side, comforting me as an anxiety attack takes over. I focus on her voice, matching my breathing to hers until I settle down. The whole thing feels like an eternity, but from what Max tells me, it only took ten minutes.

"Max, could you man the kitchen for a bit while I take Lyra up the servant staircase?" Ali asks my new friend once noticing that my breathing is under control. I smile in thanks at this amazing woman, happy that my exploration and getting lost led me to these amazing people.

"Sure thing. Don't worry, Lyra, you may be a pet, but you are also one of our own. We'll keep you as safe as we can." Max promises, his six-foot-five frame giving me a bear hug before Ali takes my hand and takes me to a hidden door behind a shelf that leads into a dimly lit staircase. The two of us climb in silence, a rule that Ali warned me before our ascent into the servant stairway. It is so that those in rooms that connected to this hidden area were not disturbed. Each step is calculated, so I do not trip in the heels strapped to my slender feet. Ali curses under her breath every so often when I trip on the uneven stone surface while helping me straighten up. This journey feels like ages as the two of us make our way in silence, me praying to beat the clock and be in the bedroom before nine o'clock. Finally, Ali pulls me to a stop on a landing and points down the hall to the right.

"At the end is the Prince's bedroom. No one is allowed to enter his room but Prince Alekai and his designated people. It's a straight path from there down to the kitchen if you ever need to get away and bake." With that, she hugs me and double-checks the basket of goodies in my arm, happy that none of the baked treats had fallen out from me tripping multiple times. I thank her once more before carefully rushing down the hallway until the sight of a door brings instant relief.

Flinging the door open upon reaching it, I come face to face with fabric, realizing instantly that this fabric is the back of the tapestry. My hidden pathway led to a well-hidden place and could be used for a perfect escape in the future.

With a grin, I carefully close the door behind me and walk out from behind the tapestry, quickly focusing on the clock and sighing with relief when I realize that I made it with fifteen minutes to spare. Placing my basket of baked treats onto a nearby table, I decide to use these fifteen minutes of freedom to explore the room I would be sharing with the Prince, deciding that the strategy of *know thy enemy* would be my best bet.

My hands run along the bookshelves, getting excited to curl into the chairs and read. But my main focus is looking for hidden passageways. Disappointed by finding none, I snoop through any area I can, opening drawers and looking under each piece of furniture and behind every painting. I'm trying to see if anything is hidden in plain sight, like a map of any kind or documents I could hold as leverage, but the search is once again futile.

With a sigh, I walk towards the only two doors I have yet to go through, wondering what was hidden there. Determined to know more about my surroundings, I fling open the doors to reveal a large walk-in closet that is three – no – four times bigger than my childhood bedroom. Split down the middle for a his and hers side, I gasp at the luxury products, some from a brand I knew all too well, Leté Fashée—Aime's family company. My throat tightens as I wonder once again about my friends' safety and if they, too, were sold into slavery, if they were looking for their freedom and trying to escape their captors as well.

"I thought I would find you here." A husky voice sounds behind me as solid arms pull me back against a sturdy chest. I know instantly who it is. It is Prince Alekai.

Chapter 6

The clock strikes nine finally, and my muscles tense in anticipation and fear. I did not hear when the Prince walked in, too absorbed in own my thoughts as I examined what I assume is my wardrobe. Silently cursing myself for my stupidity in not staying alert, I feel his hands slowly roam my body, and the smell of mint and roses tickles my nose. With each movement of his hands, the serums coursed through my body, making me overly sensitive, and I curse whoever made these horrible injections.

"Relax, Songbird, I don't plan to hurt you." Alekai whispers into my ear, gently nipping the sensitive skin between his teeth and causing me to gasp. I felt both fear and arousal, wanting to both run and hide and succumb to the heat coursing inside me. But the fear took priority. I am still a virgin who hadn't even had a first date or a boyfriend. I couldn't just let this man take what wasn't his, what I wasn't ready to give to anyone. His hands find their way to the curve of my breast, lips kissing the bare skin of my neck, and I stiffen even more, biting my lips to prevent a treacherous moan.

"If you're not going to relax, Songbird, I will just have to make you." He sighs, trailing his lips along my jaw as his hands finish groping me. Then, without warning, Prince Alekai backs away and scoops me up bridal style into his arms, causing me to cry out in surprise and grip his shirt in fear of being dropped. My eyes widen in surprise as he carries me from the closet and bypasses the large bed, instead turning towards the bathroom and carefully placing me down onto the ledge of the infinity bathtub.

"You seem like a quiet girl, Lyra, and that's fine. But I want to be the only one whose name you scream while I fuck you senseless." He states, placing a hand on either side of the tub and leaning into him. I gulp with his words, catching a passion in his eyes as I stare back at him, unsure of what to expect.

"But I want you to be comfortable and relaxed while doing so. I want you to enjoy feeling my cock deep inside you while you moan sweetly." He continues, training more kisses along my neck, causing goosebumps to form. His closeness makes me anxious, knowing that if I could not find a way to stop the course of action, he would be claiming me as his. I wanted to push him away, but with our positions, I would fall back into the water, and I did not want him to see any more of my body.

"Get undressed, now." He orders, pushing himself off the bathtub and standing straight. A smug grin is plastered on his face while he stares down at me, and I frown.

"No." I refuse, defiantly crossing my arms over my chest while I glare at him. I am met with a raised brow and an amused expression while Prince Alekai takes a step closer to me.

"That wasn't an option. Get naked now, or I will do it myself." His voice is deep, hinting at a warning in his words. I try to swallow, my mouth going dry, realizing the predicament I am in. Some form of courage or stupidity courses through me, the thought that this may be my last fighting chance to protect my innocence from this pampered manchild.

"I don't care. Nothing can make me submit to you," I declare, standing as straight as I can, even though my short frame most likely seemed like a childish feat to the tall man before me.

"If that is how you feel, Lyra, then I won't feel so bad doing this." Once again, I am lifted off the ground and thrown over Prince Alekai's shoulder. I scream in fear, clinging to any hold I can to prevent myself from falling face-first into the floor. His long legs quickly close the distance from the bathtub to the bedroom, where I find myself air-bound, landing roughly on the bed. Quickly, I scramble towards the headboard, trying to find an escape, but even at my quickest, I am too slow.

A shift in the bed alerts me to Alekai climbing onto it behind me, his hands wrapping around my ankle, pulling me close to his body, and forcing me onto my back. One hand pins my arms above my head, his lips pressing soft yet demanding kisses on my bare skin. I stifle another moan, trying to wiggle free from his grasp. His free hand slowly skims across my thigh, leaving a trail of heat in his wake until I feel him against the thin barrier of my thong that blocks his fingers from my sensitive entrance.

"I can feel you are wet, Lyra; you want me." He whispers cockily into my ear, nibbling on the skin before trailing kisses along my neck once again. His free hand slowly rubs against the thing fabric, the slight pressure making me suppress another moan. My body felt like liquid fire pooling from my core and spreading outwards. I felt dizzy and hot, with my mind turning hazy. But I had to fight.

I close my legs tightly, trying my best to prevent his fingers from moving further while doing my best to wiggle free of his grasp. His hand tightens on my wrists, causing me to wince with pain.

"Please stop!" I beg, looking into his lust-filled eyes.

"Fight and beg as much as you like, Lyra. You're mine." He answers back, ignoring my plea. He shuffles forward, using his legs to spread mine apart. I realize just how weak I am compared to this man, especially with the drug now working full force in my body. His fingers slip past the thong, slowly moving inside me, causing a moan that I can't hold back.

"See, your body is begging to be filled." He chuckles above me, his lips moving from my neck to lightly nip at my collar bone. My limbs feel weak, the fire coursing through me taking hold, and everything slowly becomes unfocused. His hand continues to work inside me, a pool of wetness now covering my thighs. Meekly, I push against Prince Alekai as his now free hand tears away the sheer dress and unclasps the bra from the front, freeing my breast and causing me to lay almost naked before him. His lips move lower, my futile attempt at pushing him away in vain as his lips encircle my erect left nipple, suckling and teasing it between his teeth. The feeling causes me to gasp as pleasure rocks through my traitorous body, and the Prince chuckles before he begins to suckle harder, breast milk flowing out. His now free hand gropes my right breast, teasing me and causing another spike of pleasure to rock through me.

"S-stop p-please!" I stutter out, my voice roars from his ministration to my body. He pulls away from my breast with another chuckle, teasingly licking the skin above my nipple.

"I don't think you want me to. Just look how wet you are." He pulls his fingers out of my soaking wet pussy, spreading his fingers to show me a film of wetness before taking the time to suck each finger clean.

"You taste as good as you sound." He groans, abruptly kissing me, forcing his tongue into my mouth where I taste my own cum on his lips. He shoves his fingers inside me, causing me to jolt and moan again, my mind cursing the drugs from the pet shop while my body loses any and all strength. The kiss is soon ended, much to my relief, as I gasp for air. I can't move; every part of me is on fire but also limp. I am helpless, and this man would soon claim me as his pet, his sex slave, at any moment. I want to cry, to scream, but the haze of pleasure is all that my mind could emotionally process in this moment. The man suckles at my right breast, teasing the nipple while drinking my milk, his fingers still working inside my soaking wet core. His well-toned body is pressed against my own, with only his clothes as a barrier between us, the only thing standing in the way of him claiming my virginity. But that soon is gone as Prince Alekai pushes away from me, removing the heels strapped to my feet and reminding me that I had something I could have used to injure the man before me. I curse my stupidity, trying and failing to move my limp body while the Prince strips himself naked. Before I can even sit up, he is once again on top of me, my legs spread before him as his lips continue their assault on my skin and breasts. His hard, lean body is pressed against my soft curve, and the tip of what I know all too well is his cock rubs against my thigh. His fingers continue working inside me, my body now moving against his hand as I feel a sensation building against my wishes.

"Look at you, enjoying every bit of this." Prince Alekai whispers against my jaw, running his lips against my cheek. I gasp as his fingers pull out of me, feeling empty inside and disgusted with myself. I know my body's reaction is from the serums injected into me, but still, I can't help but feel dirty and used with how my mind is now clouded from a lust I could not fight. Finally, the Prince pulls away from my body, a smug look in his eyes as he positions the tip of his cock against my soaking wet lips, rubbing against my entrance and making me moan loudly.

"Any last words, Lyra, before I fuck you into submission?" He asks with a chuckle. I glare at the man before me, wanting nothing more than to kill the Prince.

"Go to hell!" I growl in response, causing more chuckles from the man.

"Don't worry, little Songbird, I'll be plowing into it soon enough." With that, he thrusts inside me, causing me to scream in pain as his thick hard cock stretches me painfully. He has claimed my body as his, taking my virginity away from me. He thrusts in and out of me fast, my pussy stretched so painfully that tears flow from the corner of my eyes. His lips are everywhere, kissing, biting and sucking on any exposed skin, his arms wrapped around me, his body pressed against mine. Soon, the serums take effect again, and pleasure takes over my body in such overwhelming strength that my vision blurs, and darkness takes over.

Chapter 7

My eyes flutter open to the bright sunlight shining on my face, my body aching as I try to move as I realize I was not in my own bed. I thought that becoming a Pleasure Pet was just a dream but the events of last night flash in my mind. Prince Alekai harshly thrust his cock into me, my body moving against him as if possessed and my mind a wanton haze of pleasure. I lift the blanket, and tears fall from my eyes as I stare at my naked body, the hickeys and bite marks confirming his lips were all over me. But the glaring red stain of blood on the bed and sticky feeling on my legs confirmed that my virginity was taken by my owner. I cry silently, mourning my new life and the treatment I received last night, wondering what I should do next. Should I behave and accept my life as a pleasure pet, or should I fight and find my way to freedom? I lay in the large bed, thinking about my options while my sobs slowly die down, waiting for a sign of what to do.

"Miss Lyra." A voice calls out, and I turn my head to see Elisa standing there, a sympathetic smile on her face as she moves closer to the bed with an outstretched hand.

"Why not soak in the bath for a bit and enjoy some breakfast in the water." The Maid waits patiently for my answer, letting me decide what to do and giving me a bit of hope. I realize that even though my freedom is restricted, I can still make these small decisions for myself.

"Could we scent the water with a vanilla bubble bath?" I ask, seeing Elisa smiling wider at me.

"Of course, Miss Lyra, whatever you want!" She turns her head and gives orders to two more maids that I now see trailing behind her. I watch the ladies rush to the bathroom with a cart wafting the smell of food, which causes my stomach to growl.

"It's just us two, dear. I can help you to the bathroom after sending everyone else out." It seems like a peace offering in disguise that Elisa is sending my way, and I agree right away. The fewer people who see me in this condition, the better, in my opinion. I wait patiently, lying in bed while Elisa hums a tune and tidies the room. The two maids return and report to her, then leave, closing the doors behind them, leaving only Elisa and me in the room.

"Do you need help to stand?" Her concerned voice fills me with warmth, and I nod, slowly moving the blanket off me and sitting up with the maid's help. She lets me take a breath, readying her hands and allows me to use her as support to stand. My legs felt like jello, shaking from the sore muscles caused by last night. I whimper, leaning against Elisa with every step we took. It was a slow process to the bathroom, Elisa being patient with me as I walked carefully. The smell of vanilla tickles my nose the closer we get, and the thought of a soothing bath to help wash away the remnant of the night before brings a sense of comfort. I could not wait to wash away the events of last night from my body. My memory will be another thing to deal with altogether, though.

"Do you think you can climb into the bath by yourself?" Elisa asks as we reach the infinity tub. Again, I nod slowly, sitting on the edge of the tub and slowly placing each foot into the water before sliding myself in. I see a flicker of relief in the maid's eyes before she turns away for a moment and walks towards a cart she pushes beside the tub where I can reach, the smell of food filling my nose.

"Take your time while we clean the room. If you need anything, just call for me and I will personally come to help you." I thank her for settling into the bath and let the hot water soak my sore muscles. I hear her steps growing faint as she walks away, leaving me to myself. Although the food beside me smells heavenly, and I have a feeling that Ali had prepared it all for me, the thought of eating anything causes my stomach to churn. Instead, I close my eyes and allow the scent of vanilla to wrap around me while I let my mind wander.

∞

"Miss Lyra?" A gentle voice and someone lightly shaking my shoulder jolts me awake, water splashing everywhere from my fright. I see Elisa chuckling beside me and another maid pushing the now-cold food out the door.

"Sorry, Miss Lyra, it's just you were awfully quiet in here, and I was worried about you." She apologizes, and I sigh.

"No, I am sorry for causing a mess. I guess I am just exhausted still." I retort, leaning back against the tub and giving the maid a sad smile.

"I had a feeling that might be the case. The bed is remade with fresh linens if you want to finish washing and go back to sleep. No one would blame you for resting the whole day." She suggests, and I quickly agree. My body needed sleep, and my mind needed a quiet day to absorb everything that happened in the least twenty-four hours. Elisa runs off again, giving me privacy to wash the remains of last night from my body, finding bruises, love bites and hickeys all over my body. I felt ashamed of what happened, even though it was not my fault. I sigh, finally making my way out of the bathtub just in time for Elisa to walk in and hand me a towel to dry off.

"I figured something comfortable is needed." Elisa hands me a piece of clothing, and after unfolding it, I realize it's a long, blue cotton nightgown. I smile and quickly dress, the soft cotton feeling like a warm hug on my skin.

"Where did you find this in the closet?" I ask as she helps me exit the bathroom, and we make our way to the bedroom. The bed sits pristine and cleaned and the evidence of last night is long gone.

"In the back of your side of the closet. When you are up to it, feel free to look through your clothing," she answers, helping me climb into bed where the scent of lavender and vanilla greets me. With a clean comforter and the warm scent, I feel my eyelids grow heavy while Elisa bids me a good rest. Just before I fall into dreamland, the door to the bedroom opens, and soft footsteps come

"Is she asleep?" His deep voice is quiet, echoing around the room, causing me to panic.

"She just dozed off, your Highness," Elisa answers Prince Alekai. Shortly after, the door to the room closes, a sense of relief washing over me, thinking I am now left alone in the room. But the bed dips as someone sits behind me. I'm glad my back is towards the person as a hand gently runs through my damp hair.

"I'm sorry I hurt you, Lyra. I shouldn't have." His voice is a soft whisper as Prince Alekai apologizes to me. He must believe I am asleep while I try my best to maintain steady breathing. His hand caresses my hair while I wait patiently, too scared to fall asleep with the Prince in the room.

"You might hate me by now, and I understand that. I was an idiot. I wanted to claim you, and instead, I hurt you. I'm glad you are asleep and resting. You deserve it." His hand stops, and the weight on the bed shifts. My heart beats fast, wondering what the Prince will do to me next, but the only thing I feel is a soft kiss on my cheek before he stands from the bed. His hand again caresses my hair before I feel him tuck the blanket around me.

"Sweet dreams Little Songbird. I promise not to hurt you ever again." He whispers before his footsteps slowly fade away. The door to the room is open and shut once again, and I sigh with relief. I am finally alone, and the exhaustion takes over my perplexed mind as I fall asleep.

Chapter 8

"Lyra, would you like to come for a walk with me?" I look up from my book to see Prince Alekai closing his laptop and smiling at me. I hesitate for a moment before agreeing, marking my spot in the novel with a leather bookmark and setting it on the table beside me. Ever since his secret apology that I have a feeling I was not supposed to hear, the Prince has been kind to me. The only thing he did for the last three nights was hold me as we drifted off to sleep. Sometimes I would stay up later than the Prince, wondering what his plans were or just watching the moonlit sky from the windows. I never experienced the pain from the first night again, and his change in attitude made me question his motives.

"Where are we going?" I ask, getting up from the armchair and following him to the door.

"I figured I could give you a tour of the palace, so you don't get lost in here," is his reply. I try to walk behind him at a respectful distance as we exit the room, something I've seen other pets do, but Prince Alekai takes my hand in his and pulls me to his side.

"I can't give you a proper tour if you are behind me, Songbird." His voice is deep and husky, causing my heart to skip a beat. I nod and stay by his side, realizing my hand is still held in his. I question why he is so gentle with me now, considering his rough treatment the first day. It confuses me whenever I expect him to be harsh when I am instead met with patience and a gentle hand. The tour around the palace starts on the third floor. He explains that this floor is for us and us only, that other than a few trusted maids, no one else is allowed to enter without our permission. To say that I am shocked is an understatement. By my understanding of his words, I have control of this floor, and no one else is allowed upstairs without my permission.

"Does this mean I could have people removed from this floor if I don't want them here?" I ask tentatively.

"Yes, Lyra, this is your home too now, and I want you to be comfortable." He chuckles, pulling me closer to his body and kissing my forehead.

"You can even have a room renovated here for your own use, and if you don't want me to enter it, I won't." He continues. I have to admit, the offer is very tempting to me. He shows me three empty rooms, each with a floor-to-ceiling window, and a thought comes to mind when I see two are side by side, only separated by a wall.

"Could we renovate these two?" I ask tentatively, an idea coming to mind. I wanted a kitchen of my own, one where I could cook and bake to my heart's content without being watched by others. Maybe I could convince Ali and some others from the kitchen to join me and teach me new recipes.

"Whatever you want, Songbird, but on one condition." I frown, wondering what his conditions are and wait for the Prince to continue.

"I want you to call me by my name. Everyone else is formal towards me, including you. Can you call me Alekai, please?" It's a simple request, and I pause to think about it. I prefer to call him Prince Alekai or His Highness to keep a distance between us, seeing as the man literally bought me for his own pleasure. Calling him by his name now will make our relationship more intimate as if I agree with what he has done to me. But at the same time, the thought of having my own space away from him is tempting. With my mind made up and his expectant gaze on me, I take a deep breath and look into his eyes.

"Okay, Alekai." My answer is quiet, but I know he's heard me by the huge grin on his face and the way he hugs me tight. I blush, thinking his reaction is childish yet cute at the same time, as I hug Alekai back. It seems like I will be getting my own space as soon as I draw up a few plans for the rooms.

"Let me know what you want to do with these rooms in a few days, and I will get everything ready for you." I nod at his words, and the tour continues on. The atmosphere between us now seems warmer and lighter. Maybe we can come to an understanding soon, and I can regain my freedom. The tour continues as he leads me up the stairs to the fifth floor, explaining that this is where the King and Queen usually sleep, and he will one day have to move up here, but he prefers the third floor to himself and will most likely turn the fifth floor into rooms for his children.

We only stand by the stairs, not wanting to intrude on his parents' domain, and he brings me down to the fourth floor. This floor is usually designated for guests and extended family members. We explore the floor as he lets me walk into many of the rooms, where I realize they are designed similarly. I quickly get bored of it, and we walk down the stairs to the second floor.

"This floor is usually reserved for meetings. The congress chambers and offices are here as well as the library and other rooms meant to help rule our country." Alekai explains, leading me down the halls and mentioning that we have to be quiet as many people work here, including the captain of the guard. He leads me to the end of the hall, where the doors are wide open. I gasp at the sight of an immense library. Floor-to-ceiling shelves filled with books of every shape and size fill the room, with bright lighting from windows and many light fixtures to offer an ideal area for reading. Chairs, tables, and lounge areas are spaced out amongst the shelves for others to use, and I smile at the idea of coming here to spend my days.

"I take it you like to read." Alekai chuckles.

"When I am not cooking, painting or singing, I am reading. I love books since they can take you to anywhere you want and escape reality." I answer honestly, running my fingers along the spines of books and trying to figure out where to start reading.

"You can come back and read any time you want." Alekai chuckles, following me as I explore the library.

"Would I be punished if I miss curfew because I got lost in a book?" I ask, challenging his curfew rule. I see him frown, turning to look away from me, and I take his silence as my answer. If I miss curfew then I will surely be punished.

"The curfew is there for your safety. It's a rule for all pets, not just you. At nine, if anyone other than royal family members, guards or maids roam the palace, they get beheaded. My grandfather set this rule when I was just a child and his current pet at the time tried to use me as leverage for her freedom. She was killed. I don't want that happening to you. Being mine doesn't save you from that rule." I freeze at his explanation and turn to look at Alekai, seeing the unease in his eyes at the memory. It must have been traumatic for him. It turns out the rule was set to protect the royal family lineage, and by telling me, it's his way of protecting me.

"So, if I get caught in here reading...?"

"You'll be killed without a second thought." He answers immediately. I smile sadly and walk to where he stands, wrapping my arms around his waist and comforting the man before me.

"I'll listen to the rule then and be back by nine," I assure Alekai, feeling his tense body relax as he returns the hug.

"As long as you are on the third floor or with me, you'll be safe. I promise you this." His words spread a sense of warmth and security through me, knowing deep down that this is a promise Alekai would keep. I think I am finally starting to understand the man before me, and maybe I can let my guard down and get to know him back.

Chapter 9

I smile as I finish the last of the crown-shaped cookies, the powdered edible gold making each one shine and sparkle under the light, reminding me of the small ones Alekai has in his side of the closet as well as some vintage games that Aime, Jaida and I used to play as children. My eyes tear up as I think about my friends, wondering if I will be able to see them again and if Aime and Jaida are faring okay.

"You okay, Lyra?" Ali asked, seeing the look on my face.

"I will be. These cookies remind me of old games my friends Jaida and Aime would play as kids. I just hope that the two are okay." I answer, wiping a stray tear from my eyes, and I turn to look out the windows to the garden.

"All three of us were at a club the night I was kidnapped and turned into a slave. I wish I knew what happened to them," I add quietly, feeling arms wrap around me and Ali's scent lingering in my nose.

"Ask Prince Alekai to look into it for you. You may not see it, but we do. He treats you like more than just a pet." Ali says, giving me a reassuring smile, and I scoff.

"He treats me well because he feels bad for raping me." I correct her, watching her sigh and roll her eyes.

"Just ask him." She retorts, placing the finished cookies into a basket and motioning me to help her pack them, which I do happily.

"These go to the King's Council room. Care to come with me?" Ali asks me, taking the basket full of cookies and another filled with brownies.

"Sure!" I reply happily, following her to a different set of stairs. We talk in hushed whispers so that no one can hear us in the walls and giggle as we plan what to do for lunch. The idea of lemon chicken and fried rice is a mutual agreement as we ascend the stairs and think of other dishes to add to the meal.

We finish our conversation just as we reach the hidden door to the Council room. Ali motions me to open it, and I oblige.

"-I am not marrying someone I don't love!" I instantly recognize Alekai's voice, and he sounds furious. I flinch at the anger in his voice and pull Ali back beside me before she can walk in, motioning her to stay quiet so we can listen in.

"Well, you need a queen, and Lady Linnate fits the role perfectly." It was an older gentleman's voice, and I turned to Ali as she points at the cookies. So, this voice belongs to the King. I frown, wondering what kind of father would force his child into an arranged marriage.

"Lady Linnate is a stuck-up aristocrat who only cares about money and status. She looks down on commoners and would make a horrible queen." The name Linnate rings a bell, and I frown, realizing I had met her once when she ordered a dress from Aime's father. Lady Linnate Rushard was horrible during that appointment, even ripping apart a gown that was not the right colour of pink. This was a year and a half ago, and judging by Alekai's reasoning now, she hasn't changed one bit. Alekai is right; she would make a horrible queen.

"And I suppose this is why you bought the slave, so you can treat her like your lover and ruin the arranged marriage that I planned so painstakingly?" The King half asked, and half stated. Silence follows, and I quickly turn and run back down the stairs, not wanting to hear Alekai's response. The thought of being a tool to avoid an arranged marriage makes me furious and that the last few days of him being nice to me meant nothing other than a way to lower my guard around him.

If this is true, then that means I need to find a way to escape, and quickly. I am not a tool for others, and I refuse to become a tool once again. I do my best to keep my childhood memories at bay, leaning against a wall to take deep breaths and fight off a panic attack. I needed to calm down, focus, and not let past memories affect my thinking.

Slowly, I slide down the wall into a sitting position and focus on my breathing, finally feeling calm enough to open my eyes only to realize I am lost in the servant passageway. I frown, knowing that being stuck in here after nine at night will lead to my death, as mentioned two days ago by Alekai, and that I would have to find my way out of here, preferably back to the kitchen. Happy to have worn boots today and not heels, I stand and decide to walk down the hall in search of an exit.

I wander the hall for what seems like forever, passing vents that look into many rooms, from a laundry room to a storage closet, where I accidentally catch sight of a guard and a maid in the middle of what seems to be a steamy sex session, and quickly scamper off. It seems these walls hold many secrets that no one knows. I found no exit through my search, and I felt hopelessness seep in. I may be stuck inside these walls until a guard comes to search for those sneaking around after curfew and possibly face my death. Then I see it, a door at the end of the hall I just turned into.

I send a silent prayer to whatever deity is out there and run towards the door, smiling happily with relief when I realize it leads to the outside and a fresh breeze sweeps past me. The necklace doesn't react, and I assume I am still on the palace grounds. I walk away from the door and realize there is a hill behind me and a meadow of wildflowers before me. The scent is calming, and the stale air of the hidden passageway is washed away. I bask in the sunlight and make my way to the middle of the field, the tall grass and flowers coming to my waist. Deciding to hide away in this oasis, I find a relatively clear spot and sit down, listening to the wind and birds while thinking about what I heard with Ali. The King wants to marry off Alekai to Lady Linnate, but Alekai doesn't want to marry her. This prompted him to buy me instead. What if he chooses to make me his queen, and being a pet is only temporary?

I stay in the meadow for a while, the bells chiming every hour to announce the time, while I think about the possibility that Alekai isn't a bad guy after all, but instead just a man trying to get out of a situation he doesn't want. Unfortunately for me, I was a piece on his chess board. The bell chimes once again, signalling the noon hour and my stomach growls, reminding me that I only had breakfast and was starving. Now would be an excellent time to head back to the palace, make my way back to Ali, and maybe talk about my thoughts. With that in mind, I stand and make my way towards the hidden door I escape from, frowning when I realize it is locked. I groan in frustration, deciding to walk around the meadow until I find another part of the Palace, collecting flowers along the way until I have a large bouquet and the walls of the Palace comes into view. Of course. There are only windows and no doors, and I frown, walking along the wall. At some point, I will find a door and be able to make my way to the kitchen.

Continuing my walk, I look at my surroundings so that I can find my way back to the wildflower meadows and be able to relax in the fresh air. I spot a patio and a person sitting in a recliner; I realize it is Alekai, a book in his hand and a frown on his face. I can tell he is in a bad mood from here, but this is the only entrance to the Palace I have seen. With careful strides, I walk up the stone steps to the patio and carefully walk around him.

"Stop." I freeze, turning to face him as Alekai puts the book down on a table beside the lounge chair.

"Yes?" I ask, a little impatient as my stomach grumbles in protest of food.

"Come here." He demands, his frown still evident on his face.

"I'm not a dog."

"But you are my pet."

"I am a human being who you made a promise to." I retort defiantly, placing the bouquet on the patio table and crossing my arms over my chest. I can hear his patience wearing thin as he lets out an exasperated sigh and stares at me, his eyes holding an emotion I cannot place.

"Come here, please." Alekai pleads and I relent, seeing him so emotional and looking like a lost child. I make my way towards him, ready to stop by his side until his hand reaches for my wrist, and I am pulled into his lap. His head is buried in the crook of my neck, his lips pressed against the sensitive skin while he takes deep breaths.

"I really needed you earlier, Songbird. Where were you?" He says quietly, his voice cracking with emotion. My heart flutters, and I lean into him, feeling his hold on me tighten.

"I was helping Ali out, and when we went to deliver some treats, I got lost in the hidden passageway and found myself in a wildflower meadow." I answer, wrapping my arms around his waist and hugging Alekai back. I can feel the tension in his body slowly melt while the two of us stay in the chair, him taking deep breaths and me basking in the warmth of his hug. It is quiet and peaceful, and the moment makes me forget about my hunger as we just exist in this moment.

"So this is the slut everyone is talking about." A shrill voice calls out, breaking the peaceful moment between Alekai and me and causing him to stiffen, his grip becoming tighter as his head leaves the crook of my neck. I look to the cause of the disturbance and see a lady in fine clothes glaring at me. I glare back, intuitively knowing who the interloper is.

"Who said you can enter my private study, Lady Linnate?"

Chapter 10

"My, isn't she pretty, and her hair shines like a prism. Now I see why you bought her." Lady Linnate muses, leaning against the doorframe and completely ignoring Alekai's question. I frown and decide to play dirty, snuggling closer to Alekai and kissing his cheek to try and calm him down. I see her stiffen from the corner of my eye, and I smirk. Point for me, Zero for her.

"You!" She screeches, pointing at me.

"Me, what?" I question defiantly, placing a hand on Alekai's chest while Linnate stands there like a bird with ruffled feathers.

"Hmph, it doesn't matter." She composes herself after looking at the angry Alekai who I am snuggled into. Two points for me, zero for her.

"Enjoy your lapdog, Alekai –"

"That's Your Highness to you, Linnate!" He warns, and I see the fear in her eyes.

"Again, doesn't matter. Next month, I will be married to you while your lapdog is just that, a lapdog." She continues, and I scoff dismissively at her.

"At least I was a virgin Alekai got to claim." I say sweetly, feeling Alekai stifle a chuckle while I kiss his cheek again. I watch the anger burning inside Linnate and realize I am now her enemy number one. Good. I hate this bitch for destroying Aime's work almost two years ago, and getting back at her in any way, shape or form is something I can now do. If Alekai wanted to use me, then I would use him. Guards rush in and bow to Alekai, apologizing for allowing miss Linnate in this space, promptly dragging her away while she's kicking and screaming about how she would have their heads. I sigh, the tranquillity now ruined by her intrusion.

"I refuse to marry her." Alekai states, and I turn to look at him.

"Then who will you mar-" My question is cut short as his lips claim mine in a heated kiss. I take this as my answer and realize that the man before me plans to marry me, and my heart skips a beat. He bought me to marry me. I decide then and there to give him a chance at redeeming himself from the first night and close my eyes, kissing Alekai back with just as much passion. One moment we are making out like high school lovers on the lounge chair, the next I am pressed underneath him, laying on a sofa in his study, our clothes no longer on our bodies as his lips trail from my jaw to my neck before he pulls away.

"I need you, please." He pleads, a look of wanton need in his eyes as he holds himself back. My body is ignited with pleasure, and I nod in consent, seeing a flash of relief before his lips claim mine once again. His tongue separates my lips and slides into my mouth, where our kiss becomes a battle for dominance. I lose the battle quickly when his fingers slip into my wet pussy, causing me to gasp and moan in pleasure. My hips rock against his hand while his lips kiss and suck the skin at my neck, leading down to my breasts—sore from not expressing the breast milk yet—where he claims my right nipple, teasing and biting before finally suckling, causing breast milk to flow out and another loud moan from my lips. I feel him smirk as I look down to see him watching me, taking my breath away as he continues to the next breast, repeating the same process as his fingers continue to work their magic inside me.

Once both breasts are sore from his suckling, he continues to kiss his way down my body, nipping and sucking at my fair skin and leaving love marks until his lips bite my inner thigh. He pushes my legs apart, his fingers now leaving me feeling empty. Then his hot breath is against my core, and his tongue flicks across my sensitive skin, making me jolt with pleasure and gasp again. He is gentle as his tongue delves inside me, licking and massaging as much as he can while his hand grips my hips, preventing me from moving against him in pleasure. Pressure builds inside me, and soon I call out his name while an orgasm rocks through me, the pleasure so intense it leaves me gasping for breath.

The high wears off, and his lips are now on mine, the kiss filled with need as he grinds against the entrance of my sensitive pussy. The tip of his cock is waiting to be buried deep inside me.

"How does an orgasm feel while letting me enjoy you?" He asks after ending the kiss, his mouth against my earlobe as he nibbles on it. I moan, grinding back against him and smirking when he groans back, his body shivering in what I can only assume is pleasure.

"It makes me want more." I whisper shyly, hearing him chuckle, his body pressed against mine.

"Good, because I plan to give you what you want and take things nice and slow, Lyra." He replies, the tip of his hard cock slowly entering my slick wet pussy and making me moan. I feel my walls tighten around him, my mind becoming hazy with pleasure as he buries himself deep inside me. The air becomes heavy as we moan and groan, calling each other's names as he thrusts in and out of me, the sounds of our bodies merging as one and the calls of my orgasms loud and clear. I give in to the pleasure, my body a wanton need that he satisfies and vice versa until his lips claim mine once more in a heated kiss. My body climaxes for the umpteenth time as he stiffens above me and slams inside me once more, filling me with his seed and leaving us both panting.

Chapter 11

I yawn, feeling strong arms wrapped around me and a soft blanket covering my sore body. I open my eyes to see Alekai staring at me with a gentle smile.

"Hey, sleepyhead, feeling better?" He says, kissing my forehead and pulling me closer. I nod and snuggle closer to him while blushing, feeling a little shy from earlier.

"You fell asleep after we finished, and I just didn't have the heart to move you." He chuckles,

"Wasn't that better than the first time?" He said after a while. My stomach then chooses this moment to growl, protesting its need for food, and my blush becomes scarlet in embarrassment while Alekai lets out a deep laugh.

"I...I haven't eaten since breakfast." I mutter, turning to hide my face against the crook of his neck. Again, the man holding me securely in his arms let out another laugh, his body shaking against mine. Frustrated and embarrassed, I bite the sensitive skin on his neck, causing Alekai to freeze.

"If you keep doing that, Little Songbird, I won't be able to stop myself from devouring you again." His husky voice forces me to stop biting in retaliation, pulling away to see teeth marks and a hickey forming.

"Well then, feed me real food." I demand, staring into Alekai's eyes and seeing him looking back at me with a gentle indulgent look.

"Don't worry, I had some maids bring in food after you fell asleep. You can eat now." A kiss is placed on my cheek before his strong arms carry me to a simple table where metal domes cover what I assume to be food. After gently placing me in a soft chair, Alekai removes the domes, and the delicious scent of food envelops me. Without hesitation, I quickly dish some of the delicacies onto two plates, from grilled fish to roasted chicken and creamy mashed potatoes to sauteed vegetables. I hand a plate to Alekai, who looks at me surprised before taking a seat as well.

"Lyra." He calls out as I am taking a bite of the grilled fish.

"Yes?"

"You are welcome to come here, to my study, and relax whenever you want. If you accept it, you are the only one with full access." I look to see the Prince looking down at his food, blushing, his shy image something I have yet to see as I stare at him in amazement.

"Is anyone else allowed in here?" I ask hesitantly.

"Only Elisa and two of my personal guards. Maybe another maid or two if Elisa needs help." he nods. His explanation is simple and straightforward. Knowing that only workers are allowed in the room makes me smile, and I accept his offer. After this, the two of us finish our meal. Alekai wastes no time in scooping me into his arms and carrying me to the sofa once again, where he holds me close and cuddles me. I take this time to look around the room, intrigued by how similarly designed to the bedroom this study is.

The way to the patio on the north wall is covered with floor-to-ceiling windows, as usual, letting bright sunlight in and lighting up the room in a warm glow. The two glass doors are open wide, bringing inside the scent of wildflowers from the meadow nearby. On the south wall was his desk, and a wall of shelves with books and decorative knick knacks stylishly placed in a way that doesn't make the shelf seem crowded. The east wall is where we are, cuddling contentedly on a large sofa that could be considered a bed, if anything, a blanket covering our naked bodies. Alekai stays quiet while I explore the room with my eyes. Finally, the west wall is a small dining area, a small round table big enough to seat two people, where the remains of our late lunch wait to be cleaned off.

Finished with my exploration, I turn and snuggle closer to Alekai, as he runs his fingers through my hair gently and places soft kisses every so often. I sigh, content with the present as the exhaustion from our lovemaking and the feeling of being full slowly help me drift off to sleep. Just as I am about to fully fall asleep, the door to the study swings open and slams shut, causing me to jolt in surprise and turn to stare at the culprit.

"Your Highness, Her Majesty, your mother, sent me to remind you about the party." Elisa struts closer to where the two of us lay, a scowl on her face as she looks down at us like a disapproving mother.

"Sorry, Elisa, I am quite comfortable here." Alekai yawns, pulling me back down and tightening the blanket around us. I giggle at his childishness, feeling his fingers pinch my side shortly after.

"Your mother felt you would reject, so she asked me to pass along this message." Elisa sighs, taking out a folded letter from her apron.

"Alekai, if you do not attend the party tonight, that new pet of yours will be returned to the pet shop with clear instructions to be turned into a Breeder with a cruel, forceful breeding experience." Elisa reads the letter aloud. I shiver in fear at her words and cling to Alekai. His arms tighten possessively around me as he glares at the letter in Elisa's hand before sighing in frustration.

"Fine, I will attend the party on the condition Lyra is by my side. Prepare an outfit for her." Alekai surrenders, dismissing Elisa, who promptly leaves with a triumphant smile.

"Does she always get her way?" I ask, giggling at the pout on Alekai's face.

"With Elisa, yes. She was originally bought as a playmate for me from the pet shop I bought you from. I gave her back her freedom when I turned eighteen to thank her for being a true friend," Alekai explains, sighing as he buries his face into my hair, inhaling deeply. The news of Elisa being a slave just like me and gaining her freedom is a shock but also brings a glimmer of hope. If Elisa could regain her status as a citizen, then so can I.

"We should probably get ready before the Queen makes good on her promise to return me," I suggest, causing him to groan unwillingly and curl his body around mine.

"Let's go, Alekai." I chuckle, nudging his shoulder and trying to push his strong body off of mine. My attempts to move him are futile, as usual, and I just sigh and roll my eyes. I have a feeling this "party" is something he dreads going to and, in turn, makes me anxious to go to as well.

"If it weren't for the fact I know my mother would do as promised, I would sneak out of the palace with you." He mumbles against my hair, causing another eye roll from me before I squeal in surprise as Alekai rises to his feet and scoops me into his arms bridal style.

"Our clothes!" I call out, aware of our still-naked state.

"Trust me, no one will see us." Is his reply as he carries me towards one of the book selves.

"Pull the book that reads 'Secrets of the Heart' will you, Songbird?" I frown at his request, scanning the books and finding an old red leatherbound book, the lettering of the title etched in gold. After confirming with Alekai that this is the one and receiving a nod of approval, I pull the book only for it to get stuck halfway out, then retreat back into the bookcase, which suddenly swings inward. I stare in amazement at the secret entrance; Alekai swiftly steps inside to reveal an elevator, one I had no clue about.

"How!" I ask incredulously, getting a chuckle in return.

"I had this built ten years ago when I was sixteen. My parents went to Europe for a World Leaders' meeting and decided to stay for a month of vacation afterwards. It became a great getaway from Linnate when the lunatic tried to force her way into my room." Alekai answers, boarding the elevator and pressing the "up" button. I realize that Linnate has been after Alekai for many years and that, at twenty-six, the man holding me has built a defence system against her. Warmth fills my heart knowing that I am privileged to ride this hidden elevator, and it also gives me a quick route to his study where I can enter the wildflower meadow.

The ride is quick, and when the doors open, I am greeted by the site of the large closet in our bedroom. Again, I am shocked as Alekai steps out of the elevator and into the closet, Elisa setting out a set of clothing for each of us. I turn in his arms to look behind us just in time to watch the floor-to-ceiling mirror slide back as if nothing had changed.

"The emerald on the mirror is the mechanism to open the elevator to go down." Elisa states, chuckling at my expression.

"That's good to know." I acknowledge, feeling Alekai place me on a bench before walking in the direction of a pristine suit hanging next to a gorgeous cream gown that Elisa quickly brings to me. She ushers me to stand so she can help me get dressed quickly. The gown is silk, the cool fabric gliding across my skin as I step into it. Elisa swiftly pulls it up, guiding my arms into the sleeves, before lacing the corset at the back. I stare at myself in the mirror, amazed at the floor-length fit-and-flare ballgown with a sweetheart neckline and off-the-shoulder sleeves. The maid hands me a damp, warm towel, blushing as she does so.

"I will get the other items while you clean yourself up a bit down there." She says, causing me to blush as I realize what she means. Alekai chuckles, coming towards me with his dress shirt unbuttoned and black slacks hugging his lean legs.

"Let me help. I did make the mess after all." My blush grows deeper at his words as he takes the towel from me, gets down on one knee and lifts the hem of my dress. I jump when the towel presses against my swollen lips, stifling a moan as he quickly cleans away the remains of our lovemaking session from earlier while I fight my body and try to prevent any more juices from coming out.

"Sorry about that, Lyra." His voice is muffled from the fabric of my dress, but I have a feeling he enjoys knowing that his touch turns my body on like a dam waiting to burst. Finally, he is done helping me clean the mess away, coming out from under my dress with a smirk.

"Prince Alekai, give her a break already." Elisa scolds, rolling her eyes. After being told of their past as master and owner, Elisa treating Alekai casually with just us around seems natural. I chuckle, pushing the man towards the rest of his outfit and shooing him away from me as Elisa returns with another towel in hand. She quickly orders me to clean my face so that she can help me with my makeup.

"Shouldn't the prep team be here to do my hair and makeup?" I ask, taking the new towel and smelling cleanser in the fabric. I quickly get to work, swiping the cloth along my skin, ensuring that my face is clean and ready to be painted.

"Normally, yes, but someone instructed me that you would be attending at the last minute." She answers, glaring at Alekai.

"Now, take a seat at the vanity, Miss Lyra, so I can make you presentable in front of the King and Queen." Eilisa orders, a smile on her face.

"Um, before I sit, aren't I missing a piece of clothing." I point out hesitantly.

"No, your dress is long enough, and I don't mind you going commando." Alekai calls out before Elisa can respond.

"No, your Highness, Miss Lyra is right and needs undergarments. It would be bad if something were to happen and all the males attending saw her without any." Elisa retorts. There is a pause of silence before I hear the Prince curse under his breath, and that triumphant smirk returns to Elisa's face.

"Think you can manage to put this on without help?" She turns to me, handing me what I assume to be said "undergarments" but am quickly disappointed by the black lace thongs. With a sigh, I sit down on the bench behind me, quickly manoeuvring the fabric on and over my legs as best as I can with a ball gown on, happy when Elisa denies Alekai from helping me and forcing him to continue preparing for tonight.

Once the thong is properly on, Elisa helps me to the vanity, her skilled hands creating a natural look as the makeup has my bright blue eyes appear larger than usual. Then, quickly moving onto my hair, the Maid takes a curling iron that has been heating on the side and quickly styles the tangled mess into an elegant bun, using gem-studded pins to keep the curled locks in place and only letting a few strands frame my face.

"Now for the final touches." She giggles, her bubbly mood contagious as the excitement grows inside me. She leaves my side quickly, returning with a tray that she places on the vanity. Elisa pulls out a pair of teardrop diamond earrings, followed by a matching bracelet set. My fingers tug at the chain still around my neck, the charm with Alekai's crest a reminder that although I am attending the ball with him, I am only being paraded around as his pet no matter how well I have been treated. Elisa straps a pair of heels onto my feet as Alekai leans against the wall, watching, shaking his head while I am used as a dress-up doll for the maid's amusement.

"Close your eyes, Miss Lyra. The final part is a surprise." I oblige, closing my eyes tightly so all I can see is darkness, and wait patiently. I hear the shuffle of fabric being removed from an object, curious about what is to come, then I feel a slight weight placed upon my head.

"You can open your eyes now," she excitedly exclaims. I take a deep breath before opening my eyes and gasp at the reflection in the mirror. Placed upon my head is a dainty tiara, matching the jewelry already placed on my body. The intricate design is filled with little diamonds shimmering in the light, with the centrepiece being another teardrop diamond with a slight pinkish hue.

"Beautiful," Alekai whispers, bending down to kiss my cheek. I blush at his compliment, thanking Elisa for her amazing work.

"She is stunning. Get it right." Elisa states, shooing Alekai into another chair next to me.

"Should I style your hair with the usual, Your Highness?"

"Yes, please." With that, Elisa quickly runs a comb through Alekai's hair, his eyes never leaving my face as she creates a messy yet elegant style for his long chestnut hair, finishing the look with gel to keep the style in place and his hair out of his eyes. The final touch is a crown that matches my tiara. He stands and offers a hand to me.

"Shall we?" He asks, a playful smile on his face.

"We shall." I reply, placing my hand in his.

Chapter 12

All eyes are on Alekai and me as we arrive at the ballroom with the party already in full swing. I could see some questioning glances and hear the whispers amongst the crowd, causing me to become nervous. Moving closer to the man at my side, my hand tightens on Alekai's arm, using him as a shield from the crowd.

"Relax, Songbird, you're safe with me." He whispers and kisses my temple before we make our way to the middle of the dancefloor. I give him a tight smile, not used to being the centre of attention, and receive a chuckle in return.

"How about we dance for a bit?" Not waiting for a response, he quickly turns me around, one hand on my waist and the other grasping my free hand. Before I know it, we are moving in time to the music, dancing around the room with other couples as the swirls of fabrics blend into each other. I let out a giggle as we dance, the nerves slowly dissipating as I focus solely on Alekai before me.

"I will not leave your side tonight, I promise." He whispers after the song ends and our bodies are pressed together. I let out a relieved breath, kissing his cheek before leading him away from the dancefloor and towards the refreshment table, where we promptly receive a drink from the servant.

"Alekai, who's the cutie?" A voice calls out before an arm wraps around Alekai and a short blond man joins the two of us.

"Micho, so nice to see you." I watch as Alekai removes the man's arm from his body to pull me closer, with a glare pointed at who I assume to be his friend.

"I think Micho asked you a question." A thin, tall man with upturned eyes and long, black hair tied with a ribbon chuckles from behind Micho, causing the short man to jump in fright.

"Damn it, Yuki, why can't you be normal like the rest of us and MAKE SOME NOISE!" Micho exclaims, a hand over his heart as he too glares at the newcomer. I giggle, realizing these men are friends of Alekai, their childish behaviour something uncommon in the aristocratic circle.

"I don't think I have to answer the two of you." Alekai retorts, ignoring Micho's outburst and replying to Yuki's question.

"Oh, come on, man, we are your best buds." Micho continues, pointing into his chest and causing me to giggle. I watch as Alekai banters with his friends, wishing I could see Aime and Jaida again laughing like the three men before me. It's been a week since the three of us were abducted, and not knowing their situation causes the worry I've been holding back to boil over.

"Lyra?!" I jolt in surprise, turning to see Alekai looking at me with worry.

"I called you three times, are you okay?" He asks, pulling me closer to his body and rubbing my back gently.

"No, I'm not." My words are quiet as my fingers furl into his clothes, and I wonder if asking for his help is okay. He is my master, after all, and as a pet, I may not have the power to request things from him. I feel him stiffen beside me before stating we will be back to his friends and leading me away, the noise of the ball fading as we exit the ballroom towards a door where fresh air surrounds us.

"What's wrong, Songbird?" After wandering what I learn is a garden for a few minutes, his hand holding me close to his side as we walk, Alekai forces us to a stop and turns to face me.

"Can you find my friends?!" I blurt out, hope and pain surging inside me. I then explain the night I was taken, how Jaida, Aime and I were at the club enjoying a girls' night when I remembered going to the washroom and the world before me turning black only to wake up in the cage at the L'esclave Adoré. In the end, I find myself in his lap as I sob uncontrollably. What if Jaida and Aime were sold to horrible men? Aime is the inheritor of a fashion company, and Jaida the Heiress to her father's lands and future Duchess.

"Lyra, I don't know what you think of me, but if this bothers you so much, I will have my men look for your friends. To be honest, I am surprised you know Jaida, her father made a report about her missing a few days ago and pleading with my father to find her. Knowing she was with you that night means she was likely sold as a slave as well." He tries his best to reassure me about finding my friends as he gently wipes the tears from my face. All I can do is nod, resting my head against his shoulder, silently praying that Alekai can find and save them quickly from whatever fate they are dealing with. The two of us enjoy the garden's silence, his finger drawing soothing circles on my back to calm me down.

"Do you want to eat something and relax before we leave the ball or just leave quietly and make our way back to our room?"

"Can we go eat?"

"Of course, Songbird." His fingers trail down my cheek to my neck and rest on my collarbone, adjusting the chain. This reminds me he owns me no matter how considerate of my feelings he may be, and, honestly, the thought of being owned bothers me less and less each day I spend with Alekai as he allows me choices and freedom within the walls of the Palace. The two of us make our way back to the ballroom, the music slowly getting louder with each step. The guests are mingling happily, the socialites not bothered by their Crown Prince's departure nor our reappearance. Alekai guides me through the crowd to a set of tables where we promptly sit. A maid appears and sets two plates down before us before bowing and leaving.

"Each ball has a set dinner planned, so once a guest sits to eat, a maid will bring the food to them. The tables with green chairs are for those who are vegetarian." Alekai explains, most likely noticing my questioning gaze as we haven't ordered anything yet. I accept his answer, my stomach growling at the scent of steak, sauteed vegetables and mashed potatoes. The sound causes Alekai to chuckle as he hands me some cutlery. I accept and begin to dig in, every bite an explosion of flavour as I enjoy the scrumptious meal while Alekai quietly points out which aristocrat is which.

"Lyra?" A voice calls out, and I turn to see Duke Elyse Roland staring at me in disbelief. He rushes over as I stand, bringing me into his arms and hugging me tightly. I can feel his body shaking, my heart wrenching at the relief I can feel from the man who treated me like family all these years.

"Uncle Elyse, I-" I began, wanting to apologize for not keeping Jaida safe.

"It's okay, I heard the rumours, and I know you were bought by the Prince. Is it safe to say Jaida is facing the same fate?" the Duke asks, pulling away to look me over, sighing with relief as he must conclude that I am unharmed. I nod, tears welling in my eyes and hoping Jaida has a nice master right now and is working for her freedom.

"Duke Roland." Alekai is beside us, extending his hand to greet Uncle Elyse, never letting go of me.

"I know I have no authority to take Lyra away, but you listen to me. Prince or not, Lyra is family. If any harm comes to her, I will use every means to ruin you." He threatens Alekai.

"Don't worry. I plan to make sure Lyra lives comfortably, and as of tomorrow, my men will do everything in their power to find Lady Jaida and Miss Aime." I can see the reassurance Alekai's words cause Uncle Elys. The Duke looks at me as if silently asking whether this is true. I nod, watching as Uncle Elyse lets out a sigh and places a kiss on my forehead.

"Did you ask him to find them?"

"I did, Uncle. I may have an easy life here in the palace, but that's not to say Jaida and Aime aren't in a worse position." I answer, which seems to placate the worried father before me.

"Thank you, both of you." Uncle Elyse is called by someone after giving his thanks and telling Alekai that he can call him if he needs any help with the search. He leaves the two of us to return to our table. After seeing the Duke, my appetite has dwindled, but Alekai carries on eating.

"When did you meet Jaida Roland?" The silence between us is broken, and I smile, thinking back on the memory.

"My family wasn't a good one. My so-called father abused me, so I focused hard on getting into the boarding school outside the city. I studied hard in school, hiding my school stuff where Father couldn't find them, including applications for the academic scholarship." I smile sadly at the memory of my childhood, the bruises I covered daily at the public school while working hard to leave.

"I got the news I was accepted into the boarding school after fourth grade, excitingly telling my aunt, my mother's sister, about it. She helped me set up a bank account right away and kept it a secret from my father while the scholarship money was sent into the account. We packed up my room during the summer when Father was out at work or at the bar, and then summer ended, and I entered the school. Being from the slums, many of the kids bullied me for being a scholarship student and poor. Even my roommate made life miserable for me. After classes, I would run into the woods to find a place to cry every day, not knowing I was being followed. Then Jaida came out and sat right next to me on the ground. She said she hated how I was bullied and that her father always said talent comes from all walks of life. So she became my first ever friend. From there, I met her father, Uncle Elyse, who promptly showed me the love of a father. She had me switch to being her roommate after our first week of being friends. A month later, Jaida transferred to the school, and because of my hair, she instantly clung to me, claiming to want to use me for her fashion show." I giggle at the memory of the Aime with her aqua hair in braids, bouncing over to me before the teacher could introduce her to the class, begging me to be a model in her show. I was shy back then, instantly hiding behind Jaida for protection as the blood-haired Heiress protected me, claiming that unless she also modelled, that Aime should leave me alone. Of course, Aime agreed and would come to our room every day after the first meeting, drawing in her book. She had always been a talented designer, even at ten years old, and I couldn't help but think that meeting those two was a blessing.

"Sounds like amazing friends," Alekai observes, and I agree, looking down at my plate and realizing that I had been eating my food while talking. I smile, knowing he asked me the question to distract me. Our relationship might have started out rocky due to the circumstances, but I can tell that Alekai cares about me, and I am thankful for that.

Chapter 13

"Enjoying the food?" A shrill voice calls out behind me, causing Alekai and I to look at each other and sigh. This ball has been an eventful night that we wanted to end as quickly as possible without any more headaches. But unfortunately for us, the biggest headache of them all just placed herself before us.

"We were until your over-perfumed body made the air too toxic to breathe." I retort, pinching my nose and using a napkin to wave the air back in her direction. Lady Linnate gasps as if I seriously wronged her, her face contorted with rage.

"A lapdog like you has no right to speak to me like that!" She screeches, causing some of the guests to look our way. I shrug, turning to look at Alekai, who chuckles and kisses my cheek.

"Unfortunately for you, my Little Songbird has every right to speak to you how she pleases. You know what they say about pets, right? That they take after their owners." I want to argue with him about his remark, but in front of Lady Linnate, I have to keep the smug smile on my face and behave, even if I hate the reminder that Alekai owns me.

"Hmph, just remember that your parents want me to be your Crown Princess. Enjoy your time with your little lapdog because I plan to get rid of her once we are married."

"You have no power to get rid of me, Linnate. You're just the daughter of a Lord while I have an Uncle for a Duke." I admit, grinning, knowing that Uncle Elyse knows where I am and that he will have my back if something happens.

"My Songbird is right. I am sure Duke Roland would love to speak with your father about threatening his niece. He accepts that I own her, but he has her best interests at heart. I know that if someone sells her back to the pet store, he will use everything he can to buy her freedom." I watch as Alekai stands, ignoring Lady Linnate whose mouth opens and closes looking for words to refute our claim, but I just chuckle, taking his stretched hand and standing beside him. Knowing that Lady Linnate has no foothold to any of her claims brings some form of satisfaction to me, even if the two of us have only interacted a handful of times. Her pompous, entitled attitude rubs me the wrong way, making me want to bring her down to earth.

"If you will excuse us, Lyra and I have yet to greet my parents." With that, Alekai places his hand on the small of my back, guiding me away from our table, leaving a floundering Linnate where she stands.

"So, how do you convince your parents not to marry her?" I ask casually, watching as Alekai frowns.

"I have no clue, but I am working on it." I accept his answer, wondering if his way of working on it involves me and is why I was bought. It would make sense in a Cinderella type of story the public would eat up. A woman was kidnapped and sold as a pleasure slave for the Crown Prince; the two falling in love and, against all odds, got married. Although, I can't rule out the possibility of Stockholm syndrome since I am being held against my will. But Alekai does give me some form of freedom to do as I please.

The two of us soon quickly reach our destination, Alekai bringing me from my thoughts quickly with a kiss while we wait for the crowd before us to part. I immediately spy King Joseph and Queen Arabess, their bodies adorned in lavish clothing with crowns of gold and gems atop their heads. The Queen's long blonde hair is left to fall around her in ringlets, her emerald, green eyes, the same as Alekai's, light up the moment she spots Alekai making his way towards her, only to grow cold when they land on me. The King lazily leans against his throne, his attention on a young maid forced to stand too close, his hand carelessly groping her without the care of the public opinion. Instantly, I become wary of him. I could understand the Queen's hostility, but the King seemed like those lecherous men who ogled me at the Pet shop.

"Good evening, Mother, Father," Alekai bows, a silent reminder for me to bow as well. Being friends with Jaida has its benefits with high society as I drop into a graceful curtsy, my head bowed towards the Queen as her approval is the one I seem to need the most. I catch her shocked look as I peak from under my lashes, doing a fist bump in the air in my head. This seemed to have been the right move.

"You may rise." A deep voice states, and I obliged. I stand silently beside Alekai, waiting for their next words as Alekai gives me an approving look.

"Alekai, I did not expect you to show off your new, um, Pet tonight." Queen Arabess states, her eyes sizing me up. I smile at her, hoping to appear friendly, watching as the disdain in her eyes lessens.

"I figured since you threatened me to be here, I would bring Lyra to meet you." His answer to his mother is monotone, and the hurt in the Queen's eyes is evident. I seem to be in the middle of a family feud that Alekai has no problem dragging me into.

"Well, it seems you bought a cultured one, as she knows how to curtsy appropriately." The Queen continues, giving me an approving nod. My smile widens, and I decide to take a risk.

"If I may speak, Your Majesty?" I ask quietly, waiting for her response.

"You may." Relief fills me that the risk pays off, and I give a shallow curtsey out of respect.

"You see, I am friends with Lady Jaida Roland, and as such, I see Duke Roland as my Uncle. I was given etiquette classes alongside Jaida as children." I watch as astonishment fills Queen Arabess' eyes, and she motions me closer. Alekai gives me a light push of encouragement as I tentatively walk toward the Queen.

"I heard that Lady Jaida was missing. Is there a possibility she was captured and sold as a Pet like yourself?"

"I believe so, Your Majesty, as Jaida, our friend Aime and I were out the night before I woke up in the Pet shop. I was sold right away to Alekai, so I have no clue what happened to my friends." I answer honestly, watching the Queen nod.

"Well, if she was captured and sold, she deserved it. You females have no sense of propriety these days." My head snaps to the King, watching him chuckle in disdain at my answer while his eyes rove my body disgustingly, never looking at my face but taking in every inch of my body as if undressing me with his eyes.

"Father, if you would please, stop staring at Lyra. She is not one of your whores." I hear Alekai practically growl, his steps hurrying towards me as he brings me behind him protectively. Happy to have him block his father's view of my body, I try my best to appear smaller than I already am, not wanting to be in view of the King any longer.

"You bought her with my money, making her mine as well. This carelessness with money makes me question whether or not you are fit to be King." His father retorts, causing Alekai to chuckle darkly.

"This is where you are wrong, Father. I have many businesses under my name, including restaurants and clothing boutiques. I bought her using my own money." I catch sight of King Joseph sending a spiteful glare to Alekai's way, then catch the Queen shaking her head in exasperation. I have a feeling this is one of many conversations like this.

"So you see, Lyra is mine and mine alone. Unlike you who is unfaithful to Mother with the many whores you have lining your bed, I only have Lyra, and I plan to only have Lyra." My heart flutters at his confession, not understanding the meaning of his words at the moment. To everyone else, I was just his pet, a toy bought for his amusement, but his words seem to hold a deeper meaning.

"If you excuse us, Lyra and I will retire for the night." Alekai takes my hand, pulling me alongside him as we depart from his parents. The interaction with the Queen was not one I had pictured, but the King and his lecherous behaviour worried me. From now on, I would have to be careful not to be left alone in a room with him.

Our departure is noticed as whispers follow behind us before we exit the ballroom and make our way up the stairs in silence. I can tell Alekai is brooding, most likely over the statement his father made. It just goes to show you everyone has a home life they aren't proud of. Once we reach our room, I sit on the sofa while Alekai paces the floor.

"So, meeting your parents went swimmingly." I state sarcastically, taking my heels off and placing them on the floor beside me.

"Yeah, just peachy. Doesn't help that the monster I am forced to call Father ogled you like a piece of meat he wanted to devour." Alekai growls, taking his crown off and throwing it onto a table, running his fingers through his hair.

"To be fair, you did the same thing when I was locked in the cage." I point out, at which Alekai turns on his heels, marching towards me. He promptly sits beside me, pulling me into his lap while his mouth captures mine in a possessive kiss, his tongue pushing past my lips and plunging into my mouth, claiming and conquering me in this single movement.

"The only difference is you are mine, and I hate when he tries to take what's mine." His voice is husky as he pulls away from the breathless kiss, leaving me panting while he trails gentle bites along my neck. He smirks down at me as he pulls away, my body tingling with a need to be filled by him over and over again.

"Alekai, Lyra." I jump in surprise, seeing a bemused Elisa walk into the room as she bows at us, most likely seeing how Alekai claimed me earlier.

"Elisa, help Lyra undress and remove her makeup. I'll be in the bathroom." Alekai orders, setting me back on the couch before getting up and striding to the door.

"And Lyra, join me for a bath when she is done helping you." He pauses, saying those words before resuming his departure to the other room.

"I will." I answer, surprised by my honesty as Elisa chuckles. I glare at the Maid, watching as she winks at me before helping me to my feet. We walk into the bedroom, where she promptly removes my tiara and other jewelry, places them on the bedside table, and helps me step out of the dress.

"I am guessing the ball didn't go well." Elisa remarks, setting the dress on the bed before taking out what I assume to be makeup removal wipes from the bedside table.

"It was weird, if anything. The only bad parts were Lady Linnate and his father." I watch as Elisa frowns, asking me to keep my eyes closed as she removes the makeup from my face. I can tell that Elisa is used to Linnate and the King causing trouble for Alekai, seeing as she has grown up with him. All I can think is how horrible his childhood must have been.

"Elisa, does the king have any-"

"Pets of his own, no. He prefers to trick maids and other lowborn women into his bed. Unfortunately, the Queen has had to silence the women with money and secrecy to have them accept an abortion. I feel bad for the Queen. She deserves better." Knowing that the King has a bad habit, I can understand the Queen's hostility towards me. If I am not mistaken, she most likely wants her son to be with one woman and one woman only.

"She really does deserve better," I agree. Elisa completes her work in silence before stating I am good to go join Alekai while she finishes putting away the jewellery and dress. I thank her before heading to the bathroom, where I find Alekai leaning back in the bathtub, his eyes closed, with the scent of mint and roses filling the air. I smile, my heart wrenching to see the stressed look on his face, wondering what I could do to help him unwind.

"Come here, Lyra." His voice echoes around the room, and I oblige, walking towards the bathtub and stepping into the hot water, his hands instantly pulling me down to straddle his legs as his lips find their way to the sensitive skin on my neck.

"I need to destress with you," He groans, one hand keeping me in place while another finds its way down to the entrance of my pussy. I gasp as his fingers enter me, his lips moving to my exposed breast, where he quickly latches on, sucking and nipping at the sensitive nipple and causing breast milk to flow out. I moan, pleasure taking over while I grind into his fingers, feeling him move inside me.

"You're such a good girl, Lyra." He moans, switching his mouth to the other breast while the hand holding me in place takes my left hand, positioning it at the base of his hard cock. I gently wrap my hands around him, slowly moving my hand up and down his throbbing shaft and hearing him moan loudly. I smile, feeling accomplished as I increase my speed, massaging his cock with both hands now while his fingers work their magic inside me. I can feel myself getting closer to the edge, my hips moving faster against his fingers as I moan out his name. His free hand tangles into my hair, pulling my face towards his, where he claims me in a hungry kiss, our tongues in a tango of dominance. As I feel the walls of my pussy tighten, ready to feel the sweet pleasures of an orgasm, he pulls away, a smirk on his lips while I whimper at the loss and frustration of not cumming

"I never did get to punish you for getting lost in the Palace. What if you had stayed out past nine." He chuckles out, licking the skin of my neck while making me shiver.

"But I still made my way back to you." I argue meekly, getting another chuckle from the man before me.

"That may be so, but you deserve to be punished, and I know the best one." With that, Alekai stands from the bath, stepping out before lifting me into his arms. I am carried to the bed, where he promptly throws me onto the mattress before climbing in after me.

My legs are soon spread wide apart, his thick hard cock being plunged into my already soaking wet pussy as he thrusts in and out of me at a punishing speed. I call his name out in pleasure, grinding my hips alongside his thrusts as I reach the peak of pleasure, ready to be thrown over the edge. But before my orgasm comes, Alekai pulls out, one hand placed on my neck loosely to keep me down while the other strokes his cock. I whimper, begging him to let me cum, but he just chuckles, waiting for me to whither underneath him before once again thrusting deep inside me, filling me with his hot cum. I moan both in pleasure and frustration as the process repeats, his cock thrusting hard and fast inside me, only to be pulled out of me right before I can cum. He continues rotating between stroking himself and thrusting into me until the next time he is inside me, he fills me with his cum once more. His lips are on my skin, kissing, licking and biting, leaving a trail of marks for all to see if I wear a low-cut top.

It isn't until late in the night, when his energy is spent and I ay away in his arms trying to find some form of sweet relief, that I realize just how much power the man sleeping beside me has over my body.

Chapter 14

"She tripped me for fun when I walked by her on my way to Alekai's library," I exclaim, answering Ali's question about what happened a few moments ago as she hands me a bag of ice for my throbbing ankle. A week has passed since the ball, and my life has become one of avoiding the King whenever I spy him in the hallways or having a battle of wits with Lady Linnate—one that I always managed to win—or avoiding her and her flying monkeys completely when she is in a group.

Today, the crazy woman caught me off guard as I made my way to the library, her foot coming out of nowhere and causing me to fall down a few steps. Luckily, Ali and Max had just finished serving Queen Arabess, and my fall was stopped by Max, who luckily caught me. Taking the bag of ice from my friend, I gingerly place it onto my ankle, gasping and whimpering from the pain as I fight back the tears. When I see Linnate next, her face will have to undergo plastic surgery to fix what I plan to do to her.

"I think your ankle might be broken, Lyra." Ali sighs, turning around to write onto a notepad before motioning to one of the new kitchen maids.

"Take this to Prince Alekai in his study or Maid Elisa if you see her first. If anyone tries to stop you, say this concerns Lyra." My friend orders, the kitchen maid nodding in understanding before taking off as fast as she can through the hidden stairways.

"One of these days, I will be able to navigate those hallways without getting lost." I sigh enviously, only to cry out in pain as I accidentally move my foot, pain shooting through every nerve ending like a jagged knife.

"For now, let's focus on helping you to the hospital wing of the Palace. When you are better, I will have Neena help you learn the hidden stairways." My friend says with concern, checking on my swollen ankle. She carefully removes the bag of ice, my vision growing black from the pain as she puts slight pressure on the injury, most likely trying to figure out how bad it is. All I want to do at that moment is throw something at her, the pain becoming so unbearable that it takes everything in me not to pass out.

"Didn't she try to pour wine on your dress yesterday when you and Elisa went to the Prince's study?" A small voice asks from my left, and I see Neena, Ali's fifteen-year-old daughter, enter with a bouquet of flowers in her arms.

"Yes, Linnate has it out for Lyra because she stands in her way of the Crown's money." This has been the main topic of our discussions for the past few days since Ali heard the gossip of Linnate becoming the next Queen. Unfortunately for her, the servants all hate her, and many have come to me, revealing they secretly hope that I beat all odds and take the throne with Alekai. I just roll my eyes at Ali's explanation, letting out a gasp of pain when someone touches my ankle, and it takes everything in me not to kick poor Neena. As much as the girl has become like a sister to me since she started working in the kitchen five days ago, there are times like this when I want to tie her to a chair and leave her there.

"Neena, don't make Lyra's injury worse!" Ali scolds, pulling her daughter away from me and directing the fifteen-year-old to the decorator's side, where Neena is forced to help decorate cookies for the Palace residents to consume.

"Thank you, she was one more poke away from being hit. Hard, might I add." I sigh, happy to only have Ali beside me.

"Where is she?!" A frantic voice calls out as the doors to the kitchen slam open, causing me to jump in fright before the stabbing pain blurs my vision, causing tears to fall. Couldn't people be a lot more careful with an injured person in the room?

"Lyra, I am so sorry, baby. Are you okay?" To my relief and frustration, the person who barged into the room was Alekai. The Prince quickly makes his way to my side and wipes away my tears.

"We think she might have broken her ankle. Linnate tripped her down the stairs when she was on her way to the library. Luckily, Max and I had arrived just in time as Max caught her and prevented further injuries."

"This is the third incident where Lyra has gotten hurt because of Linnate." Alekai seethes in frustration, taking the ice pack off of my ankle and handing it to Ali. I cry out in pain the moment he lifts my foot to carefully examine it.

"Al-Alekai, please s-stop! It hurts." I beg, clutching his arm as I start to sob from the pain. Slowly, he puts my foot back onto the chair it's been resting on, moving beside me to wipe more tears from my face and kiss my forehead.

"I'm sorry, Lyra. I never meant to hurt you." he coos, wrapping me in his arms and allowing me to sob the pain out as Ali replaces the bag of ice. I bury my face into his chest, taking in his now-familiar scent of roses and mint while focusing on my breathing. The pain slowly settles down to a tolerable level before I pull away and look at Alekai, whose face holds worry and concern for me.

"Are you ready to be moved to the hospital wing?" He asks. I nod, not trusting myself to speak right now as I focus on keeping my foot still so as not to further aggravate the injury to my ankle. Alekai presses a kiss to my forehead before untangling me from his arms and standing, slowly taking his time to lift the ice bag from my ankle and putting it on the table beside me and gingerly lifting me into his arms.

"Bite down on my shirt if you have to." He whispers as my face scrunches up with pain when my foot moves ever so slightly. Once again, I bury my face into his chest, my hands clenching his shirt as silent streams of tears begin to flow. I can tell that he is being careful with me as he begins to walk in what I assume is the direction of the hospital wing, mindful not to move my foot too much. His steps are rushed but measured, and the pain is bearable to a point, only surging when he has to turn a corner into a new hallway.

"Almost there." I hear him say after what feels like an eternity. A wave of dizziness washes over me as I feel his body shift, and a maid apologizes for nearly knocking into us. I bite down on his shirt, pushing closer to his sturdy chest and praying this walk will be over soon. I don't know how long I can fight the pain before I faint. Finally, the smell of rubbing alcohol reaches my nose, and Alekai slows his pace.

"Doctor Ridley, that snake came after my Little Songbird again!" Alekai exclaims, the sound of his footsteps echoing in the quiet room as I feel him gingerly place me onto a bed, making sure to cradle my very swollen ankle as a nurse comes with a pillow to rest my foot on.

"What did Linnate do to you this time?" Doctor Ridley, an elderly man with a full head of grey hair and a clean-shaven face, asks as he enters the main room from his office. I sigh in relief, knowing that my pain will be gone soon with his expert healing.

"She tripped me on the stairs when I was on my way to the library. I think I broke my ankle because of her." I answer quietly, clinging onto Alekai, who moves to sit beside me on the bed. I watch as the Doctor sighs, a look of exasperation on his face, the same one he had when I first met him six days ago. At that time, Linnate had managed to convince a maid to put a potent itching powder on my jacket when I wasn't looking. The feeling of my skin becoming so unbearably itchy to the point my scratching caused some bleeding is one I will never forget. Alekai found me in a sobbing mess when I never showed up for lunch. He quickly wrapped a blanket around me and carried me to the hospital wing, where Doctor Ridley prepared a bath in minutes and made me soak inside, clothes and all, for an hour before having a maid remove the fabric from me, and Alekai placing me into another bath.

I watch as the Doctor shoos the nurse away. He gingerly runs his fingers around my injured ankle, causing me to cry and cling closer to Alekai, who does his best to calm me during the examination.

"It's not broken, but badly sprained. I am guessing you don't have much pain tolerance?" Doctor Ridley says after removing my shoes. I feel so relieved knowing I won't have to undergo surgery to fix a broken ankle.

"No, I don't. My father abused me as a child, and ever since then, I can't handle pain." I answer honestly, feeling Alekai stiffen beside me.

"I expected as much. Kai, carry her into the next room, and I will be right there."

"Yes, Doc." I feel strong arms once again lift me bridal style, Alekai taking his time to carry me to a side door leading to what I refer to as the spa treatment room. The walls are painted a calming blue, and natural light coming in through the tinted windows gives the area a soft glow. On the west side sat comfortable chairs with foot baths placed in front, ready to be used for treatment, while on the east sat three tubs for soaking in medicinal baths. Alekai turns towards the chairs, sitting down and helping me sit facing the foot bath, his arms wrapped around my waist and holding me close. Doctor Ridley soon walks in, a large jar full of blue liquid in his arms.

"Place your foot in the tub, please." He motions to the foot bath, water slowly bubbling. With Alekai's help, I slowly place my foot into the soothing water. I breathe a sigh of relief as the warm water helps with the throbbing pain. I watch as he pours the contents of the jar into the water, the tingling sense of medicine working quickly as the pain dulls.

"Keep your foot in there for an hour. I will come back to check on it. Feel free to put your other foot in, as the medicine will also help strengthen it," Doctor Ridley orders. Before I could agree, he is already out the door, most likely going back to his office to make a formal complaint about Linnate injuring those in the Palace again.

"An hour alone sounds like a fun time," Alekai whispers, his hands moving my hair off to the side as his lips press against my neck, kissing me softly.

"But I can't move. " I whisper, clutching the arms of the chair as his hands slip around to fondle my breasts.

"That's okay. I can just play with you while you sit like a good girl." He nips my neck, and I moan, leaning into him, my body slowly becoming aroused as his hands and lips work their magic on my body, and his fingers slip under my skirt. Since we will be alone for an hour, we might as well enjoy a distraction from the pain.

Chapter 15

"A-Alekai!" I moan my master's name as an orgasm rocks my body. His fingers continue to massage my twitching pussy, causing me to gasp before he removes his fingers from inside me and brings them to his lips, sucking them clean of my cum. I blush knowing that my thighs, his lap and the chair are a mess from his *special massage*, as he puts it. I am left a breathless mess as I lean against his chest, feeling a bulge against my backside. I just know that Alekai is moments away from plunging himself deep inside me.

"You still taste delicious." He whispers, nibbling my ear with his arms now wrapped around me. My blush deepens, and he chuckles, the bulge in his pants rubbing against me, giving me an idea for some petty revenge. With a smirk, I slowly wiggle against Alekai, feeling his arms stiffen around my waist as he groans.

"Doc said to stay still, Lyra." He mumbles, my smirk becoming a smile as I continue to wiggle, feeling his hands instantly move to my hips, forcing me to stop moving.

"Keep doing that, and I am punishing you later, Songbird." He growls through a groan, causing me to giggle as I realize I, too, have power over this brooding yet caring Crown Prince.

"As long as that punishment doesn't bring her back here, then have fun." Doctor Ridley's voice rings out as he enters the room and comes to a stop by the foot bath, where he promptly turns it off and takes out my injured foot, carefully moving it up and down to test my ankle sprain.

"How does it feel?"

"Better than before the injury. The pain is gone too!" I answer.

"That's good, Lyra. Want to try walking on it?" He suggests. I nod, allowing the doc to put my foot back into the water before carefully taking both feet out and drying them with a towel. Then, using the arms of the chair, I rise to my feet and test my weight on the ankle before taking a few steps. I take the time to balance on the foot that was injured, smiling triumphantly when there is no pain before walking towards Doctor Ridley again.

"It feels better than before the injury. Whatever that medicine was, it's amazing."

"Good, now try to keep out of Linnate's path or else I will have to keep a room here just for you."

"In my defence, Doctor, Linnate hunts me like a bloodhound chasing a deer. Even when I do everything to avoid her, she sniffs me out. I think she has a bigger obsession with me than she does Alekai." I defend myself, hearing Alekai chuckle as he wraps his arms around my waist and pulls me close.

"I will make sure she stays out of trouble, Doc. Besides, Linnate will be in serious trouble for what she did today." Alekai reassures, kissing my forehead while I roll my eyes. We bid goodbye to Doctor Ridley, Alekai leading me towards the back of the room where a wall fountain quietly bubbles, pushing a button and leading me through a hidden passageway. Hand in hand, we walk in silence, the two of us just enjoying each other's company. I peak into the vents, looking into the rooms we can view, some full of servants while some are empty. One room catches my eye, and I tug Alekai's hand, motioning him to take a peek.

Inside, his friend Yuki was busy with a maid, the image of a prim and proper lord now gone.

"Why, I'll be damned. Macho is going to love this," Alekai whispers, taking out his phone to, I presume, take a picture of Yuki in the act before quickly putting it away. After this brief pause, we continue on our walk until I find myself pressed against the wall, my face turning towards a vent I recognize as the one inside the Council room. Alekai's lips are soon on mine, his hand groping my breasts harshly.

"I said I would punish you for teasing me at the doctor's office." Alekai whispers against my neck, trailing kisses down to my collarbone. I do my best to suppress my moan, my eyes looking into the Council room where Queen Arabess and King Joseph sit side by side, their stewards and council listening to a tanned man talking about the planning for this year's harvest.

"Lyra, you are not to make a sound, do you understand?" Alekai whispers into my ear, biting the sensitive skin while I hold in a moan. I nod in understanding, lust filling my body once again as I hear the zipper to his pants slowly come undone. The anticipation of Alekai soon deep inside me causes my need for him to grow. I feel myself being lifted into the air as Alekai nudges my thong to the side and oh so painfully slowly pushes the tip of his hard cock inside me, his lips on the crook of my neck, biting the sensitive skin. I close my eyes, biting my lip and forcing myself to stay silent as he enters me, grinding his hips as his cock fills me. I want to moan, be loud and let him hear how much he affects me, but I stay silent, knowing the people on the other side of this vent could hear me the moment I give in. He gently pulls out, my body shivering and toes curling as I dig my nails into his shoulder, wanting nothing more than for us to find a more private area so he can devour me there instead. He continues his slow, steady thrusts, grinding inside me and ravaging my neck with his kisses and nibbles, my body craving more from him.

"I don't think you are enjoying this, Lyra." Alekai whispers seductively into my ear, causing me to shiver as I grind against his cock that's once again deep inside me, my eyes pleading with him silently for more. He chuckles, forcing my face forward before capturing my lips in a passionate kiss. His tongue dances with mine before the kiss ends too quickly for my liking, and my face is once again pushed to face the vent.

"I really want to hear you, Lyra. Hear how much you enjoy feeling every inch of me devour you." Alekai continues, gently pulling out of me until just the tip remains. And then, without warning, he thrusts hard and fast inside, his cock moving in and out, punishing my soaking wet pussy and hitting deep inside me until I succumb to the pleasure, and a moan escapes my lips.

"What was that?" A voice calls out inside the conference room. I suddenly feel a pair of lips on mine, Alekai forcing me to stay quiet as his mouth devours me in a kiss.

"Probably a guard fucking one of the maids. It happens from time to time." The King's reply resonates in my foggy mind while Alekai thrusts harder and faster inside me until I feel my insides find sweet release, and I cum, my moan swallowed by Alekai's kiss as he stiffens, his hot sticky cum filling me.

"Guess you will be punished more tonight, Little Songbird." He whispers triumphantly, holding my body closer to him as I try to catch my breath.

"Think you can stand for a moment while I pull my pants up?" I hear the concern in his voice, taking a moment to think before I hesitantly nod yes. His chest rumbles against mine in amusement as he slowly pulls his now limp cock out of me, the sensation causing me to whimper into his shoulder with light pleasure before I untangle my legs from around his waist and set my feet on the ground. I carefully lean against the wall, my legs unsteady, feeling like jello, as Alekai quickly pulls his paints up and pulls me into his arms once more.

"Are you hungry, Lyra?" Alekai asks, pushing a strand of hair behind my ear. My stomach makes its presence known as a loud gurgle comes out from me. I blush, burying my face into his chest and nod, not trusting myself to make any noise right now after the moan I let out earlier. He chuckles again, his fingers playing with my hair.

"Do you think you can walk?" I shake my head no at his question, my jello-like legs slightly shaking. If it weren't for his arms being wrapped around me or the wall I leaned on earlier, I would have already crumbled to the ground.

"Can you carry me?" I quietly ask, gaining another one of Alekai's deep chuckles.

"Of course, Songbird." I smile as his arms quickly scoop me close to him, my arms automatically wrapping around his neck while I rest my head against his shoulder. His scent of roses and mint wraps around me, and the soft sound of his heart beating starts lulling me to sleep.

"Tired?"

"Yes." I mumble, yawning as my eyes close. The walk is a comfortable quiet, Alekai carrying me through every twist and turn as I drift in and out of sleep. To think, just two weeks ago, I was terrified of this man. Now, all I want is for the chain to be removed from my neck and actually get to know Alekai for who he is. A door opens, and before I fall asleep, I see that we have arrived at Alekai's study.

Chapter 16

"Is she awake?" A soft voice asks. I frown, snuggling closer to the pillow underneath me and praying that whoever is ruining my sleep leaves. A chuckle from beside me answers the question before a hand slowly plays with my hair.

"I think she is Elisa. Can you bring us some food?" I sigh, realizing that my slumber is now over and slowly open my eyes to an amused-looking Alekai.

"Hi." He chuckles, leaning forward and kissing my forehead.

"Hi." I yawn, snuggling closer to the pillow and pulling the blanket closer to me.

"How long was I asleep for?" I ask, closing my eyes as Alekai continues to play with my hair.

"About an hour. You fell asleep just as we arrived at the study. So, I decided to let you rest even though you were hungry and figured we could eat when you woke up." I smile at his thoughtfulness, feeling his hand stop as I am scooped up again in his arms before settling in his lap.

"So, what have you been doing while I sleep?" I ask, snuggling close to the Prince and scanning the table beside us. I realize that he must have moved the small dining table closer to the couch where I slept. My heart skips a beat knowing that Alekai moved it to be closer to me.

"I have a charity ball tomorrow night. Duke Roland and I have been collaborating to create a new high school where the students can learn real-life skills such as a trade or artistic talent. It will be part-school, part-business, where the students can sell their work to help build their brand and find a job once they graduate. A way to help the economy grow." Something in my mind clicks, and I think back to three months ago, back at Uncle Elyse's estate. Aime, Jaida and I were called into Uncle Elyse's study, where the Duke explained that he would be busy for the next few weeks as he finalized a project that we were told would bring many children a better future. I remember being curious about this project, wanting to know more and see if I could help. But Uncle Elyse shooed me out with the other two, saying we would know more when the time was right. I guess the time is right now.

Elisa returns, pushing a cart of food into the room. Another maid quickly gathers Alekai's paperwork and piles it neatly onto the empty chair I should be sitting in. Still, Alekai tightens his hold on me, and I give in, staying in his lap as two plates are set before us, each with a simple chicken bacon sandwich and french-fries that smell heavenly to my protesting stomach. I quickly dig in, feeding Alekai a fry from my plate while I enjoy the sandwich, the crispy lettuce and hot, grilled chicken. This is just what I need after a long day.

"When did you and Uncle Elyse come up with this project?" I ask, taking the time to finally learn about this important project that piqued my interest months ago.

"Two years ago. As you know, I have created many businesses over the years, some being restaurants." I nod, taking a sip of the milkshake that Alekai hands me, my attention solely on him.

"Well, Duke Roland is a partner in one of my businesses, a construction business. We both agreed we needed to find a way to hire talented individuals." Alekai answers. From there, he explains that the school was originally a trade school for high schoolers. In this place, kids who worked better with physical learning over academic learning could enroll and gain experience that would land them a career in construction upon graduation. But then it evolved because Uncle Elyse mentioned that construction was not the only business the two men owned. Of course, each year would offer the traditional courses in mathematics, English and so forth, but would also include a variety of classes from construction to baking and even fashion and arts.

"When Duke Roland mentioned a girl his daughter was friends with and her dream of becoming a baker, I agreed right away to make the school encompass other trades and fields."

"I'm that girl." I whisper in awe, realizing why Uncle Elyse kept this project a surprise.

"You're that girl. It wasn't until the ball last week and piecing together what I have learned about you that I realized you were the talented girl he gushed about as if you were his own daughter." Alekai confirms, smiling as he brushes away a few crumbs from my lips with his fingers.

"So the party for the school is tomorrow?" I continue, excited to see this project that is partially inspired by my own childhood.

"Yes, and it will be held at the school. I already have your gown picked out." My lips form a broad smile, excitement at a new environment other than the Palace and a chance to see Uncle Elyse again. Elisa returned to clear our empty plates as Alekai accepted the paperwork from earlier, handing me the pile to look through. I am quickly absorbed into the words, the plan of action laid out over the last few years from the school's location, if it would be a boarding school or not, and how many buildings would be there. I can't help but admire Alekai and Uncle Elyse more, smiling when I realize there are specific buildings for specific trades. My favourite is the culinary building.

"Have you named the halls yet?" I ask, finding the school's blueprint and wishing this had been my own.

"Each one will be named after trees. Apple Orchard is for culinary, Weeping Willow for construction, which includes electrician and woodworking trades, and Sakura for the arts. We are thinking of Spruce Forest for the student housing but feel we should have separate names for the female and male dorms." Alekai answers, his fingers pointing out each building on the sheet. I stay silent, wondering what a good name would be before pointing to the male dorms.

"Keep this one as Spruce Forest." I say before pointing towards the female dorms.

"And this one Plum Orchard."

"Why Plum?" I giggle at his question before pointing at the wall closest to the female dorms.

"If I am not mistaken, this school is close to the largest fruit farm, and the plum orchard is right by the female dorms. Why not talk with the owner of the farms to allow collaboration with the school where students can learn about farming? We need more of that in this kingdom, with the lands charred from the war slowly being recultivated. You could even waive land tax for the first five years if the graduates become farmers and cultivate their own fields." I continue, voicing the suggestion I believe would help strengthen the country and reduce food costs.

"That's an amazing idea, Lyra! How did I not think about this!" Alekai exclaims before his lips capture mine in a quick kiss that ends too soon as the door to his study bursts open, and an irate man stalks towards us with guards on his trail trying to stop him. His piercing gaze is like daggers as he focuses solely on Alekai.

"Alekai, you bastard! Why haven't you been spending time with your fiancée?!" The man screams, his fists swinging towards Alekai and subsequently me. But luckily, a guard tackles this man to the ground, apologizing profusely to Alekai and me as another comes to help detain this stranger.

"Nole, I do not have a fiancée." Alekai's voice is as cold as ice as he sends Nole a glare that would kill if possible.

"Liar! Linnate is your fiancée, she said so herself!" The man named Nole screams like a rabid animal, trying his best to fight off the two guards pulling him back.

"I never agreed to that arrangement. In fact, I despise your sister. I wish someone would marry that whore already so I can be rid of her." Alekai spews in disgust, pulling me closer to his body and kissing my forehead. I could feel the glares of hatred from Nole, and I already despise the man who thinks he can just burst into Alekai's study without permission. He is nothing compared to my Prince, and if it weren't for political reasons, I have a feeling Nole would have been killed by now.

"If anyone is the whore, it's that slut on your lap/" Nole spits out, only to be slapped by a guard.

"Get this straight, Nole. Lyra is no whore. If anything, she belongs to me and only me because I was her first and will be her one and only." I blush at Alekai's words, motioning for the guards to take Nole away. With a guard on either side, dragging the dishevelled man out the door kicking and screaming, I sigh in exasperation, now realizing that I have to guard myself against Linnate and her brother Nole. The door is left open, the screams of Nole's complaints echoing down the halls until silence.

"The first thing I will do as King is strip that whole family of their titles." Alekai mumbles, his arms shaking as he pulls me closer once more. My hand wraps around his back, slowly drawing circles to help calm him down.

"Prince Alekai, Miss Lyra." Elisa's voice calls out as the sound of a door closing catches my attention. I turn my head slightly to see Elisa waiting patiently by the door for Alekai to respond.

"Can you tell Nick to ready the car for us, Elisa? Lyra has been trapped here for two weeks, and after Nole's unwanted visit, we both need some fresh air."

Alekai orders. Elisa bows, leaving just as quickly as she came once again as Alekai loosens his hold on me. His eyes hold fury, one I know is directed at the siblings who keep causing trouble for us. The stress is evident on his face. I smile reassuringly at Alekai, pulling his head closer to mine and kissing him gently.

"Everything will be fine, Alekai." I whisper once we pull away.

"I know, Songbird." He answers back, kissing the top of my head. Elisa enters once again, informing us that the car is ready. Alekai thanks her before leading me out of his study and down the halls. This would be my first outing since being sold as a slave, and I cannot wait. Maybe I can use this time to convince Alekai to set me free and get to know each other on more equal footing.

Chapter 17

The car is waiting outside the Palace entrance, with the driver I first met after being sold to Alekai waiting patiently for us. He looks my way, a frown evident on his face, before turning to Alekai.

"Pardon my meddling, Your Highness, but are you sure this slave won't try to run? She did think to try it when you brought her home."

"Don't worry, Nick. I trust Lyra and know she will stay by my side." Alekai answers, helping me into the car as I roll my eyes. But Alekai is right; I wanted to stay with him. Besides, even if I try to run, my necklace will inject a serum into my body, and the tracking device would alert Alekai and the Guards to my location. I would need this collar off if I ever decided to run away. I slide into the seat, settling in comfortably for the ride as Alekai slides in beside me, wrapping an arm around my waist and pulling me to his side.

"So, where are we going?" I ask, snuggling close to him as the car comes to life and begins to make its way out of the Palace grounds.

"It's a surprise," is the answer I get, with Alekai closing his eyes. I once again roll my eyes, deciding to watch the view outside as the Palace gates open. I catch glimpses of the outside world once again since being sold. The world looked the same, as if three ladies being taken and sold had never happened two weeks ago. Through the streets, I could see the fruit stand where I would shop, the café owned by Mrs. Laila where I would grab my breakfast from in the morning, and the park I would take a walk through. Sadness swells inside me, thinking about the life I had before being kidnapped, sold, and wondering if I would ever be able to do those mundane things I used to do again.

Then fear replaced the sadness as soon as the car turned onto a familiar road.

"You... You're not taking me back, are you?" I hate how small I sound as I cling to Alekai, turning to look at the man as the car slowly drives closer to L'esclave Adoré. I can vividly remember the poor girl being bred and the customers wanting to breed with me as well. I know that as my owner, Alekai could sell me back, and my fate would be in the Shop owner's hands. I would do anything to avoid that fate.

"No, Lyra, I am not taking you back there." Alekai reassures me while running his fingers through my hair. I still felt unease, the fear still strong inside me as I move closer to him, refusing to let go. This causes Alekai to sigh, his hand now fisting my hair and tilting my head to look at him again.

"How about I prove to you that you aren't going anywhere?" He whispers, his voice gaining a husky undertone as his lips capture mine in a heated kiss. His hand leaves my hair, moving down to my waist as he quickly scoops me onto his lap, forcing me to kneel with his lap in between my legs. I can already feel his need for me, the bulge in his groin rubbing into me as I slowly relax and grind into him. Our tongs battle for dominance while the kiss deepens, his hands sliding down my waist and to my ass, where he promptly spanks me, causing me to jolt and gasp with surprise.

The kiss ends as we pull apart, gasping for breath. His lips continue to pepper my cheek, chin and neck with little pecks before ending at my collarbone, making me moan while Alekai kisses, bites and sucks the sensitive skin. I can feel my body growing needy, wanting to feel him deep inside me once more as I move faster against his bulge, grinding and rubbing against the main before me.

"Now, do you believe you are mine, and I refuse to give you up?" He whispers into my ear, biting the lobe.

"Yes!" I moan. I am pushed onto my back on the seat, Alekai quickly pulling my thongs off and pushing my skirt up. His pants are now unbuttoned, and his cock stands at attention, stiff and ready to be buried inside me. It isn't long until Alekai positions himself at my entrance, his cock slowly pushing inside my soaking wet pussy, and another loud moan leaves my lips as I feel every inch pressed against me. The car ride soon becomes filled with our moans and gasps, Alekai thrusting into me hard and fast, his lips and hands leaving a burning trail of need in their wake where ever he touches me until the two of us finish, his hot cum filling me as my walls squeeze around him.

By now, we are far from the city, and my worries of being sent back to L'esclave Adoré are long gone. I was Alekai's, and nothing will change that. I will never be sold or harmed as long as I am with this man, whether as his Lover or Sex

Slave, and the realization that I accept this notion calms me. I will never have to fight for my life again and would be protected by this man.

"Alekai," I whisper, wrapping my arms around his neck and pulling him closer to my body.

"Yes, Lyra?"

"Will you take this collar off of me one day? I promise I'll never leave your side." I ask, smiling softly at the man above me. I see his hesitation as he thinks about my words, letting out a long sigh as he buries his face in the crook of my neck.

"I can't promise anything, Lyra, but I will take it off of you one day." He answers, placing a soft kiss on my neck and taking a deep breath. His words fill me with a tiny spark of hope. It isn't a promise, but knowing he plans to take this necklace off of me eventually is enough for now. I will regain my freedom eventually.

Chapter 18

Alekai and I lay cuddling in the car's back seat, his arms holding me tightly to him as I play with his hair. His eyes are closed lightly, and I smile as he dozes off. The last few days, I have noticed how tired he has been, knowing now that it was for unveiling a new school that will help the future of the Kingdom. The car continues along the road, and I stare out the window, wondering what surprise Alekai has for me. The city is long gone, and nothing but farmland and crops fill my view. The simplicity of it is breathtaking and quaint. Time passes, with Alekai still dozing and me watching the scenery until the car turns onto a simple dirt road and slows down to a stop in front of a large farmhouse.

"Alekai, I think we are here," I whisper, shaking him slightly. He groans and mumbles something under his breath, his arms hugging me tighter. I chuckle, enjoying his childish behaviour and shake his shoulders once more.

"Alekai, wake up." I call out slightly louder, feeling the man holding me stir until his eyes slowly open and a yawn escapes his lips.

"Are we there yet?" He mumbles, rubbing his eyes, and I giggle.

"You tell me, considering you never told me where we are going." is my retort, gaining an eye roll in an un-princely manner. He sighs, letting go of me and pushing himself up into a sitting position, looking out the window as a large grin spreads across his face.

"Yeah, we are here." His chuckle makes me smile as I sit up, taking a better look at the farmhouse while smoothing out my clothes, Alekai taking the time to button his pants and give me a once over, making sure both of us look presentable.

"You ready for your surprise now?" His question excites me, and I nod, excited to stretch my legs, breathe in the fresh country air, and find out what we are doing here. He chuckles again, running his fingers through his hair one last time before opening the door, exiting the vehicle before offering a hand out to me that I graciously take and—with his help—exit the vehicle. Nick is leaning against the driver's door, a lit cigarette in hand as he nods at us respectfully. Alekai leads me towards the back and as we grow closer, the distinct sounds of puppies reach my ears, and a giddy feeling rises inside me.

"Are those...?" I ask excitedly, stopping in my tracks at the prospect of owning a pet.

"Why don't you go and see?" With his permission, I smile and quickly release Alekai's hand, running the rest of the way to where the sound is coming from, seeing a pen full of puppies of different colours exploring the backyard.

"So, do you like your surprise?" Alekai comes up behind me, wrapping an arm around my waist as I watch the fluffy creatures chase after one another.

"I love it! I was never allowed to own a pet growing up. I had planned to adopt one, maybe a cat, once my studies were finished." I answer happily, noticing a small white puppy ignored by all but one of their littermates.

"Your Highness, glad to see you came!" A voice calls out, and a man comes walking towards us from a building just slightly off to the right, with six large dogs trailing behind him.

"Thank you, Jones. As I mentioned earlier, I wanted to bring my girlfriend here for a gift. Do you have any recommendations?" I listen as Alekai takes the lead, my eyes still on the two pups, a white one with fur that shimmers in the light and a pure black one that shields her from the other pups that try to bully her.

"Well, as you know, our wolfdogs are popular with the nobles, so I would suggest one of the largest of the litters we have. All are twelve weeks old and ready to go." Jones, the man who I assume is the breeder states, and I frown. The two pups that have caught my attention were outcasts, that much I can tell, and as wolfdogs, they would not survive in the pack.

"What do you do with the runts and outcasts?" I ask, watching a larger wolfdog walk over to the two pups and growl at the black one for biting a grey pup that tried to attack the white one.

"We sell those for cheap to the nobles or to other farmers as farm dogs. But most of the time, we find them dead because of the pack's animosity to them." He states plainly. I frown at his answer, walking away from the two and carefully scooping the black and white pups into my arms, doing my best not to startle them as I notice a surprised look on Jones' face and an amused smile on Alekai's.

"I'll take these two." I state, determined to keep these two pups from any harm.

"Are... Are you sure?" Jones asks, perplexed by my statement.

"Very. They need a good home, and I plan to give them one." I stare adamantly at the breeder before looking at Alekai, hoping he will say yes to this.

"I did say this is your surprise, and if those two are what you want, then we'll take them, Lyra." A grin spreads across my face as Alekai consents, and I look down at the pups in my hands, both staring at me with bright blue eyes.

"If you insist, I will sell them to you at the regular discount. By the way, these two are from completely different litters if you wish to breed them." I look up at the two men, happy to know that my surprise is something I wanted as a child and wonder if Alekai already knew this about me. He is a business partner with Uncle Elyse, and in the Duke's house, it was common knowledge that I wanted a pet.

Alekai leaves with the man to pay for the wolfdog pups in my arms while I decide to sit on the grass, petting the two new members of my family. I start pondering the possibility of breeding my own wolfdog pack if I want to and realize that Alekai had called me his girlfriend to Jones.

"Ready to go?" Alekai calls out, snapping my attention to him.

"Yes. Thank you for the surprise." I carefully stand, keeping the two pups in my arms and make my way to where Alekai stands, wrapping an arm around my shoulders and kissing my forehead.

"Why don't we head home then and get these two settled in." I nod and lean into his embrace as we walk back to the car.

"I see she didn't run away," Nick states the moment I step into view.

"Why would I? I have a home and a boyfriend." I snap back, my statement causing Alekai to chuckle.

"That's right, and I have a girlfriend." He agrees, kissing my forehead once more and helping me into the car. Nick grumbles something under his breath. I ignore the man; instead, I settle the pups onto the seat beside me as Alekai climbs in and closes the door before the car drives away and back home.

"Any idea on what to call these two?" He asks, and I turn to look at the now-sleeping pups.

"Nova for the little white girl and Chaos for the little black boy."

Chapter 19

"Alekai, what do you want to do when we get home?" I ask, yawning as I watch the passing fields outside the window.

"Did you just say home?" Ignoring my question, Alekai slips a finger under my chin, making me look at his shocked expression.

"Yes. The Palace is my home, isn't it, since I am your pet." I state the obvious, wondering why Alekai looks shocked. His brows furl, and I catch a glimpse of what must be either guilt or regret in his eyes before he looks away from me and runs a hand through his hair.

"I have a meeting to go to when we return, so you can take Nova and Chaos to the study and stay there. Elisa should have finished bringing the pet beds and toys in there." He replies, and I nod, snuggling into his side and enjoying his arm wrapped around me.

"When your meeting is done, why don't we head to the wildflower field with the pups and have a picnic?" I suggest. Some intuition tells me that Alekai is not looking forward to this meeting, and if my hunch is correct, it has something to do with his father trying to arrange his marriage.

"I'd like that. I have no idea when the meeting will end, but stay inside the study, for now. Elisa will stay with you until I can." I look up to see him staring at me with a gentle smile, and I nod, leaning up to kiss his chin.

"Sounds like a plan," I whisper, getting a chuckle as he hugs me, kissing the top of my head. The car ride is left in peaceful silence, the two of us just enjoying each other's presence.

"Can I ask you something?" I break the silence a few moments later, pulling away to look at Alekai.

"You just did." He chuckles, causing me to roll my eyes at him for the umpteenth time today.

"I am going to take that as a yes. My real question is, why do you call me Songbird?" I ask. Since being sold to the man before me, Alekai has always called me by my name or the nickname given to me.

"Your voice is exceptionally beautiful and captivating. If you wanted, you could have been an Idol instead of a chef."

"Baker." I corrected, getting a chuckle from Alekai.

"Baker. Either way, you are my Songbird, a beautiful creature with a beautiful voice." I blush, happy with his answer, as I curl back into his side. The ride returns to a comfortable silence, the engine's hum the only sound. The city skyline comes into view, reminding me how close to home we are, and the thought of curling in bed with Nova and Chaos makes me smile. Being kidnapped and sold was a horrible experience, but meeting Alekai has given me a better life than I could imagine. I have ample food, a bed I can sleep in every night and friends here. I do still want to find Aime and Jaida and see them happy and healthy.

"I have a question." Alekai's voice breaks the silence. Curious, I turn to look at him, learning he is already staring at me.

"What is it?"

"Why haven't you given me a nickname yet?" I can see his easy-going smile waver, his eyes betraying the mask of happiness he put on to prevent me from seeing the hurt and unease inside them.

"I never thought of giving you one," I answer honestly, seeing the disappointment seep through as he looks away.

"Is it because you hate me? Because I bought you?" His voice is a low whisper, and my heart clenches at his sad tone. Do I hate Alekai? Not anymore. Yes, he bought and raped me the first day we met, but he's more than made up for his actions in these two weeks. His caring attitude and worry towards me is something no one other than Jaida, Aime, and their fathers have shown me.

"Alekai, I don't hate you, not anymore." I reach out and cup the other side of his face, gently turning his face towards me, the hurt in his eyes evident.

"You used to hate me?" He asks, sounding like a lost child.

"I did, especially after you raped me." I wouldn't lie to him, lying has caused too many problems for people, and I refused to allow a lie to hurt us. Alekai wants to pull away, I can tell by the way he tries to let go of my waist, but I cling to him, wrapping my arms around his waist and leaning into his body.

"Don't pull away, please. Like I said, I used to hate you, but your actions have shown how much you care for me. Without knowing it, I ended up liking to spend my time with you, liking you for you." I pull Alekai closer, seeing the hurt in his eyes disappear, replaced by warmth. He leans closer, his lips taking mine in a slow, gentle kiss. My heart flutters with every second. His lips move softly against mine, his arms drawing me closer, to the point our bodies merged against each other as near as possible despite our clothes being in the way. I felt safe, cared for, and... Loved.

"I can wait for the nickname, Lyra. I can wait for as long as it takes. But I want to know what I am to you." His voice is husky from the desire I can see he is holding back as Alekai states his intentions. At first, I am taken aback, but then I begin to think. What is Alekai to me? I know he owns me, but I have never felt like his property or slave since the first night, and I even referred to him as my boyfriend earlier—mainly to annoy Nick. Yet, I have no clue what he is to me.

"I don't have an answer to that yet. Could you give me some time?" I reply quietly, resting my head against his chest and listening to his steady heartbeat.

"Of course, Songbird. Like I said, I can wait." I nod, turning to kiss the spot over his heart while his hands gently play with my hair, happy to know that Alekai wouldn't rush me while I figure things out. Maybe I could regain my freedom once I decide what he is to me. The car slows to a stop, and I look out the window to see we have arrived.

"This outing was too short." He grumbles, and I agree, letting go of Alekai so that he can climb out of the vehicle first while I scoop the pups into my arms and slide out of the car myself.

"Lyra, I have a meeting in thirty minutes. Will you be able to head to the study by yourself?"

"Yes, I should be fine." I answer, Alekai placing a hand on the small of my back and walking with me to the Palace doors.

"That's good. Elisa has everything for Chaos and Nova in there. Promise me you will stay in there."

"I promise." With my reassurance, Alekai quickly pecks my cheek before rushing away down the hall to the right. I sigh, turning in the other direction and walking towards Alekai's study. Along the way, I am stopped by a few court ladies and maids who coo over the black and white puppies in my arms. I proudly inform them that Alekai bought the wolfdogs for me. Soon the whole Palace will know Alekai bought me some pets. I have a feeling this will destroy Linnate's self-esteem. Good.

Reaching the safety of the study, I nod to the guards who greet me amicably, opening the door to the study and allowing me entry. Once inside, I spot Elisa with a smile on her face, setting down a large, fluffy dog bed. Puppy toys are scattered across the floor, from chew toys to ropes, tennis balls, and even a few stuffed animals. Beside the table where Alekai and I usually eat are two sets of dishes, with puppy food and water already inside.

"This looks amazing Elisa. Thank you." I call out in awe, placing the pups on the floor and watching the two instantly sniff around the room, Nova finding the stuffed animal that she instantly starts to cuddle with.

"Thank you, there is more in your bedroom for these two," Elisa answers. Chaos walks towards the maid and places a ball at her feet. I smile as I watch her bend down, pick the ball up and toss it across the room, Chaos bounding after it with a yip.

"What are their names?" She asks as I come to stand beside her, watching the pups explore and play.

"Nova is the white one. She is a female. Chaos is a male, the little black one who brought the ball to you."

"Same litter?"

"No, they're from different litters, which would make it easy to breed them in the future."

"Do you think I could have a pup if you breed the two?" I turn to face the Maid, her eyes never leaving the pups, with a longing I knew all too well.

"Of course, you can have the first pick. They are wolfdogs and have wolf instinct, so I hope you can handle the responsibility." I agree immediately. Elisa turns to me and hugs me in excitement.

"I took care of Alekai; I think I can handle a wolfdog pup." She retorts, causing the two of us to laugh. It's strange to think that the Maid and I had a rough start, me finding her to be more like a prison warden at the time. But now I know Elisa is loyal and has become a great confidant and friend.

"Would you like to stay and play with us?" I ask, seeing a sad look cross her face as she walks to the table and picks up two collars, one pink and one red.

"I would love to and I know Alekai wants me to stay with you, but I have to serve the meeting, the King ordered it and neither Alekai nor I can go against a royal order." She answers sadly, handing me the collars as she turns to look at the pups one last time.

"How about you watch the pups when Alekai and I are unable to? It can be part of your duties, and you can play and cuddle them." I suggest. I watch as the sad look on her face turns into a happy smile.

"I'd love that. Thank you, Lyra." She agrees wholeheartedly, turning to pet Nova who now drags a stuffed unicorn plushie towards the bed. Elisa stays for a moment, promising to have their name tags with Alekai's crest delivered later tonight. Before bidding us farewell, she reminds me there is a cart of snacks to enjoy while I wait. Now alone in the room, I open the large doors to the deck, grab a bag of small dog treats and head outside, calling for the pups to follow me and feeling happy when they do. I will have to start training them to be great pets and guard dogs for myself. Alekai not only gave me pets but also a way to protect myself when alone in the Palace.

Chapter 20

Some time passes, and the afternoon sky from earlier held pink, blue, orange, and red streaks as the sun began to set a while ago. I was happy to spend the time training Chaos and Nova after getting their collars on, teaching the two their names right away, and teaching them to come to me when I call their names, allowing the pups to roam around the deck and grass nearby. At first, I called them at the same time, and I rewarded the pups with a treat as soon as they arrived at my feet. Eventually, I started calling them one by one, calling out to Chaos first and rewarding him when he came, before doing the same to Nova.

A chilly gust of wind has me shivering, and I call out to the pups one last time, Nova in the lead, while I slowly walk back to the doors and wait for Chaos, who joins us soon after, a stick clutched in his mouth. I chuckle, holding out a treat to both pups. Chaos quickly trades the stick for the treat before I pick the two up and bring them inside, placing them on their bed before rushing to close the doors. I did not need these two running out without being trained.

My stomach makes itself known then, growling from hunger as I take a look at the time—seven o'clock in the evening. The meeting should be done soon, but I decide to snack on what was left behind by Elisa, rolling the cart to the couch. I promptly plop onto the cushion, exhausted from the exciting day, and reach for the platter of fruits waiting to be eaten. Deciding to pass the rest of the time waiting by reading, I pick up the book I left on the side table and curl up, the book in one hand while the other reaches for the fruit I happily munch on.

ço

"Good book, Lyra?" I jump in surprise at the voice, just as the clock on the wall finishes chiming eight times. I had gotten absorbed in the romance novel, not hearing the door open. But the door that opened was not the main door, but the one leading outside. I quickly stand and turn to face the voice, noticing Nole standing there with a smirk on his face.

"Sorry for my intrusion and rude behaviour earlier, Lyra." Nole begins, walking towards me. I quickly walk towards the table, keeping furniture between Nole and I. His presence here is suspicious. From the corner of my eye, I see Chaos and Nova watching Nole intently, the two staying silent but reminding me of their presence and that wolfdogs are incredibly loyal to their owners.

"Thank you for your apology, Nole, but the one you should apologize to is Prince Alekai, who is on his way back from the meeting." I state, focusing on the man as he slowly creeps towards me, his smirk growing.

"I know he is in the meeting. My father is the one who requested it." Nole states, and I nod. The meeting most likely has to do with Alekai not marrying Linnate like her family wants.

"Well then, you should know you are trespassing in the Prince's study and should not be here. Leave this instant before the guards come." I continue, backing towards the shelf on the right. The second time I came to his study, Alekai taught me where the emergency button is to call the guards. Everyone would think it is on the desk, but it is actually the crest on the bookshelf, Alekai's crest.

"No can do, Lyra. I am here to send a message to Alekai. The first message is to kill you, of course, after having my way and enjoying Alekai's whore. Then, with you out of the way, Alekai will have no choice but to marry my sister as planned." Nole lets out a dark chuckle, pushing the furniture to the side and lunging at me. I quickly turn and sprint to the bookshelf, pressing down on the crest and feeling relieved when the wolf's eyes turn red. Two minutes and help will be here, I think, turning just in time to dodge Nole as he slams into the bookshelf, objects and books falling over and onto the floor. But my escape is short-lived as he grabs my hair from behind me, pulling me back into his body, with his left hand wrapping around my neck.

"Now, now, Lyra. You're a sex slave and should be doing your job properly." He whispers into my ear, his tongue licking the flesh. I shiver in disgust but do my best to free myself by elbowing Nole in the stomach. He winces, and his grip loosens enough for me to turn and punch him in the face, dazing the man and taking the chance to run to the main entrance of the room. But whelps of pain cause me to turn around to see Chaos being kicked away while Nova bites into Nole's ankle, blood already dripping from the wound.

"So the rumour is true. He bought you pets of your own." Nole chuckles darkly, shaking off Nova, who growls at Nole. I quickly run towards Chaos, the puppy lying on the floor by the table growling at Nole, but I am grabbed, this time being pushed into the table and falling onto the floor, Nole pressed on top of me.

"You are such a handful." He seethes, pinning my hands above my hand with his right hand while his left hand slides under my shirt to grope my breast. I can feel the bulge in his pants as he grinds against me, his hand moving from my breasts to tug my skirt up, his fingers pushing past my thong and into my pussy. "See, you want it. You're already wet, you filthy whore." He states, his finger working inside me, causing the serums to work and making my body burn for more. But I wanted none of it.

"Someone help!" I scream, tears falling from my eyes while I focus hard on resisting the effects of the serum and fighting to escape.

"Shut the hell up." He barks out, punching the side of my face and causing my vision to blur, but I ignore him and scream as if I am being murdered, screaming at the top of my lungs, waiting for someone to hear.

"I SAID SHUT-" a loud crash is heard behind us, guards rushing into the room surrounding Nole and I.

"Hands in the air!" Someone yells, Noel quickly obliging as his hands leave me. A guard holsters his gun before pulling Nole off of me, another covering me in a blanket and helping me sit up. My throat is sore from screaming, my head pounding from the punch earlier, but knowing the guards came on time has relief filling me.

"Lyra!" I hear his voice before his warm arms wrap around me, Alekai's scent filling my nose. I sob into his chest, finally feeling safe as his hand runs through my hair.

"I am so sorry, Songbird." He whispers, pulling me closer, his apology causing me to sob harder. He has nothing to apologize for. It wasn't Alekai's fault for me being attacked. But still, I had just missed the narrow reach of being raped and killed by a man who would do anything to see his sister become the next Queen. My sobs turn to whimpers as I catch my breath, Alekai sitting on the floor and shifting me to his lap.

"What do I do with the pups?" Someone calls out, a guard holding Chaos and Nova in his arms.

"Are they injured?" I ask quietly, gently pulling away from Alekai and reaching out to them.

"Thankfully, no. They might be bruised but no broken bones and no other injuries." The guard answers, and I nod, Alekai allowing the man to place my puppies in my lap. I gently pet them, reassuring myself that they are indeed uninjured, and thank what ever guardian angel is watching me for keeping my pups safe.

"They attacked Nole for me. Nova even drew blood." I state, happy to know my pets were okay.

"That's why I got them for you. Maybe we should get a few more and have a small army of wolfdogs to protect you." Alekai chuckles, petting Chaos gently. I think about his words and agree, but only on the condition that I get the runts and outcasts of the litters. We watch as the guards search Nole, two holding him down while two ruffle through his clothes. A pile of knives is already forming on the ground beside them. Meanwhile, disgust is filling me because that vile man touched me.

"Miss Lyra, I hate to say this, but you have a black eye forming." The guard that brought my puppies to me states sheepishly, looking towards Alekai wearily,

"He hit you?!" Alekai shouts in alarm, gently turning my face to see the damage done.

"He was going to rape and kill me, Kai, so you can marry Linnate with me out of the picture." I state, shivering while I lean into him more, his arms tightening protectively around me.

"Adam," Alekai growls, his body shaking.

"Yes, Your Highness?" Adam, the guard who handed me Chaos and Nova, answers obediently.

"You will be assigned to guard Lyra from now on when I am not with her." Alekai orders. I smile, looking up to see the rage in his eyes, but the concern for my well-being trumps the rage.

"Understood. Besides, she gave us a reason to arrest this bastard." Adam answers, chuckling as he turns to watch the search. It seems to be over as the two guards holding Nole down have now hauled him to his feet, putting handcuffs around his wrists while another collects the weapons Nole hid on him. Each small knife would have been used on me if I hadn't pressed the emergency button.

"Adam, can you carry the pups to our room while I carry Lyra?"

"Of course, Prince Alekai." With that, Alekai passes Nova and Chaos to Adam, scooping me into his arms before standing. A guard informs us that they will take Nole to the dungeon and deal with him accordingly, and Alekai just nods before exiting the room, me in his arms and Adam trailing behind us.

"Is it safe to say our picnic is cancelled?" I ask quietly, trying to break the tense silence.

"For now, yes. We can have one tomorrow." Alekai answers. I nod, allowing him to be protective and hoping his anger will dissipate. I know his anger is directed at Nole for attacking me, but being near an angry man causes my nerves to be frazzled. Reaching our room, Adam sets the pups on their bed in the living room before excusing himself. Alekai carries me straight into the bathroom. Settled on the edge of the tub, Alekai helps me to remove my clothes before guiding me into the warm water, the scent of roses and mint filling my nose before he climbs in after me.

"Tonight, we can just relax. I'll make a brief appearance at the party being hosted tomorrow and then come home to you." He says after sitting in silence for a while, his hands slowly helping me clean.

"I want you," I state, turning to face Alekai, ignoring his suggestion of relaxing.

"Lyra, you were nearly raped and killed!" He argues, the loofah in his hand dropping into the water as his arms pull me back against him. His body starts to shake, and something wet falls onto my shoulders, making me turn around and see that Alekai is crying. Instantly, I wrap my arms around him, holding Alekai tight.

"I'm here, though, Kai. You and the guards saved me."

"You could have died. I could have lost you!"

"But I am here, and right now, I need you, need some normalcy." I retort, kissing his cheek. He pulls away, his tear-filled eyes taking me in before his lips claim mine in a passionate kiss, one I relish while his hands slowly skim across my body, memorizing every inch and curve, causing me to moan.

The kiss ends all too soon with Alekai climbing out of the bathtub before scooping me into his arms, the both of us dripping wet without a care for the mess. He carries me to the bedroom, gently laying me on the bed and climbing between my legs, his lips hungrily leaving trails of kisses and bite marks, the stress from earlier melting away with his touch. I needed him, wanted him, and I would get him.

Without warning, I shove Alekai off of me and onto his back, taking the time to straddle him as my lips start their own assault. I kiss every inch I can, leaving a trail of hickeys and bite marks on every visible part that clothes can't hide as well as ones that only we will know, like his stomach and thighs, all the while my hand slowly caressing his thick, hard cock. Alekai is mine, just like I am his, and I would be dammed if I let another woman touch him.

"Do you want to try something different?" His voice is husky, a low moan ending the question. I smile, happy to see the effect I have on him.

"Good, move closer to my cock, Lyra." He orders. I oblige, trailing my kisses back up his body until I claim his lips. His hands are on either side of my hips, his tongue battling with mine while he continues to guide me to a better position until the tip of his cock is pressed against my soaking pussy.

"Slowly lower yourself onto me." He grunts, one hand leaving my hip to hold his shaft in place.

"Are you sure I won't hurt you?" I ask, a little unsure.

"Trust me, Songbird, I'll be feeling amazing." He laughs, causing me to blush. I decide to take things slow, carefully lowering myself where only the tip of his cock enters me before grinding slowly.

"Fuck!" He groans out in a shaky whisper under his breath. I smirk, continuing to lower myself onto him with his guidance, letting out my own moan as I realize just how deep inside he is while straddling him. I continue to grind against him, his cock moving slowly inside me, making my walls twitch.

"Now, slowly move up." He orders, his hands back on my hips, digging into the skin. It takes everything in me to move, lifting my body slowly off of him as his cock glides out, more moans escaping the both of us until just the tip is in. And then I repeat, slowly riding his cock as every time he fills me brings me closer to the edge. He suddenly thrusts up, causing me to gasp and fall onto his chest as my walls contract around his cock, and I cum, calling out his name in ecstasy.

"Now it's my turn to have fun." Alekai chuckles, and within a blink of an eye, I find myself on my back, legs wrapped around Alekai as he devours my body, reminding me that I belong to him.

Chapter 21

I groan as sunlight falls on my eyes, waking me from my dreams. Warm arms hold me protectively against a warm body, and I smile as I open my eyes to see Alekai sleeping blissfully, a soft smile on his face. I lay there, watching him sleep. A month has passed since Nole tried to rape and murder me; his trial ended in his execution yesterday afternoon. Linnate and her family have been banned from entering the Palace for a year unless for official business, meaning I would no longer have to see that whore as often as I used to. The Palace feels safe for me to roam the halls again, no longer worried if Linnate and her flying monkeys would try something on me when I run into them.

"Good morning, Lyra." A deep voice calls out, and I notice Alekai looking at me.

"Good morning, Kai." I reply, leaning forward and placing a light kiss on his lips. I can't help but smile as I snuggle closer into his arms, hearing him chuckle as his hand plays with my hair.

"How long have you been up?" He asks, and I sigh.

"Not too long, maybe thirty minutes. I left you to sleep because you need it." And the truth is he does. Since the night Nole broke into the study, Alekai has been training the guards and improving the Palace's security, being gone all day and arriving late at night, sneaking into bed. I spent those days with Ali in the kitchen, Adam trailing behind me with the pups in his arms while I cooked and baked with my friend, or in the redesigned study training Chaos and Nova and returning to my room at curfew as always, falling asleep with only the pups to cuddle. If it weren't for his side of the bed being messy and warm from the nights before waking or being woken up in the middle of the night with Alekai teasing me until I screamed his name in pleasure, I would have thought Alekai was staying up late and neglecting his sleep.

"Thanks for that, beautiful. I forgot to mention that tomorrow is a charity ball my mother is hosting. I have your dress delivered today for you to try on, with me beside you, of course." I roll my eyes at his innuendo, pushing Alekai away playfully. After the attack, I had gotten my menstruation, happy to know that all the sex with Alekai did not lead to a baby.

"You're free today?" I ask, making sure.

"After a quick meeting at noon, I am all yours after two in the afternoon." I smile at his words, already planning a picnic surprise that we never got the chance to have yet.

"Do you think you can meet me in the study then?"

"Of course." He kisses my forehead gently, resting his chin on the top of my head and taking a deep breath as we lay in bed, talking about what I have been up to the last few days before the clock chimes the time and forces us to get ready for the day.

"I have a surprise for you, Lyra, before I have to prepare for the meeting," Alekai states as I tug a sweater over my head. The weather in the capital is becoming cooler, signalling fall is on its way.

"What's the surprise?" I ask, throwing my hair into a messy bun. He smirks, motioning me to his side where he promptly kisses me passionately, his tongue sweeping across my lips, prying for access, which I give. I moan, my body starting to heat up and the feeling of need growing, but he ends the kiss with a chuckle pulling away and wrapping his arms around me.

"This is a reminder of what I want to do tonight with you." He whispers seductively before taking my hand and leading me out the room, me cursing his teasing and the serums that altered my genetics. I thought that the effects would have worn off, but a conversation with Doc the day after the assault proved me wrong. The serum given to slaves, especially those meant for sex and pleasure, was designed by a scientist when the trading business picked up. It alters the DNA of the recipient and will last for a lifetime.

I follow Alekai, the short walk ending in front of a door that leads to empty rooms.

"What's this?" I ask, staring at the door skeptically.

"Your surprise, go take a look." Under Alekai's encouragement and expectant gaze, I slowly turn the handle and open the door, gasping when I see inside. A gleaming, brand new kitchen with marble countertops and perfect appliances greeted me, a large fridge with what I hope is filled with ingredients sitting just to the left of the kitchen. Taking a step in, I notice the wall connected to the adjoining room is gone. Instead, a lounge with bookshelves, sofas and chairs greets me, and a small fire in the stone fireplace adds warmth.

"It took a lot of work keeping this from you after you explained what you wanted. I will admit I asked Duke Roland for help with the design." Alekai states, and I shriek happily, turning and hugging the man.

"I love it. Kai, this is amazing!" He chuckles, hugging me back before letting me go to explore the room, noticing two dog beds placed under a window where warm sunlight filters in.

"Elisa has the pups right now. She should be bringing them back soon." As if on cue, the sound of barking comes down the hallway before Chaos and Nova bound inside the room, circling Alekai and I.

"Oh good, you showed her this room," Elisa states, her uniform slightly dishevelled, some mud splattered on the hem in the shape of paws.

"Yes, I did. Now I have a meeting to get to." With that, Alekai gives me one last kiss before walking out of the room, Elisa coming to stand with me as I admire the room again.

"Have you ever baked cookies?" I asked the Maid, seeing her shake her head no. With a grin, I take her hand, pulling her towards the kitchen, where I promptly get her to wash her hands. I was in a baking mood, and with this new kitchen of my own, I'd be damned not to use it.

ထ

"Something smells good in here." I turn to the open door to see Alekai leaning against the frame, eyes closed as he takes a deep breath of the air. I chuckle, close the lid to the picnic basket stuffed with goodies, and turn to look at the clock. Elisa and I have spent the day baking. Adam arrived an hour after Alekai left but spent the time playing with the wolfdogs. Of course, he relished in the fruits of Elisa's and my labour, taking treats from the cooling racks and sharing some with the dogs with my permission.

"Thank you. Elisa and I baked all day." I reply, motioning to Elisa, who sat on a couch with a sleeping Nova in her lap while Chaos played tug-o-war with Adam.

"Lyra is a great teacher, and the treats are amazing." Elisa chimes in, Adam chuckling as he shoves a cookie into his mouth.

"Well, I am free now, Songbird. Anything you have in mind?" Alekai chuckles out, making his way towards me, where he places a kiss on my lips.

"Actually, yes. Elisa and Adam are going to watch Chaos and Nova while we go on a date." I retort, taking the picnic basket in hand before grabbing Alekai's arm and dragging him towards the door, a bemused smile on his face.

"Have fun, you two!" Adam calls out just as we leave, and I chuckle. Alekai allows me to lead him down the stairs and towards his study. This picnic was long overdue, and I would not allow anyone to disturb us. Once in his study, my steps falter before continuing to the doors leading to the patio. My grip on Alekai tightens as the memories of what happened here flash before my eyes, causing me to shiver. Since that night when Nole attacked me, I haven't been able to step inside. And so I rush to open the doors, happy when the fresh air hits my face.

"I plan to have my study moved." Alekai says, closing the doors.

"Why?" I ask, turning to look at him.

"Because working in here without you sucks. I know you don't feel safe there anymore, and I want to give you a safe home." My heart melts at his explanation, and I smile, leaning in and planting a kiss on his jaw.

"How about we renovate it instead? This is the only way towards the wildflowers, and I don't want to lose them." He readily agrees to my suggestion, making me feel blissfully happy knowing that Alekai has my best interest at heart. It makes me feel like his one and only; how I wish I could make that happen. But he is a Prince, and I his slave. We would have to fix this status in order to have a real relationship. With a silent sigh, Alekai and I make our way to the wildflower field, where the scent of the flowers relaxes me. Setting the basket down, I take out the blanket from the basket and hand it to Alekai, who promptly sets it on the ground for us to lay on, and with that, the picnic commences.

"So, what was the meeting about?" I ask casually, taking out the bowls of food and setting them between us on the blanket.

"The usual. Father wants to arrange a marriage for me, and Mother is trying to push Linnate as a candidate. They finally stopped when I threatened to renounce my claim to the throne." He chuckles at the end, taking a snickerdoodle and biting into it, moaning as he chews.

"Jesus, they weren't kidding about your skills. These are amazing." I blush at his outburst, happy to know that Alekai enjoys my baking as the two of us begin to eat, Alekai peppering me with praises for the sandwiches, cookies, pies, and pigs in a blanket.

"I feel like if I ate your food every day, I'd gain weight and become a fat Prince." Alekai whispers as we lay on the blanket, the dirty dishes packed away in the basket. The breeze makes the tall wildflowers sway, and the warm sunshine in the early fall air keeps us warm.

"Well, maybe you shouldn't have built that kitchen." I jokingly say, poking his stomach and getting a chuckle out of him.

"But seeing you so happy was worth it, Lyra. You deserve the best." I blush at his words, snuggling into his side and sighing. Moments like these make me wish we were a normal couple on a date, not a slave and master.

"I forgot to tell you that tomorrow is a charity ball. Linnate and her family will be there, but I was hoping you'd be my date." I lift my head in surprise, looking at Alekai who looks away sheepishly, a blush forming on his face. Is my Prince shy? I wonder, my heart fluttering.

"Of course, I'll be your date, Kai." I happily answer, tilting his face towards me with my free hand and kissing him gently.

"That's good. There is no other girl I want beside me." For some reason, I feel like his words hold a deeper meaning.

Chapter 22

"You look amazing," Alekai states as he walks into the closet, just as Elisa helps me into my heels.

"The dress is so flimsy, though," I complain, rolling my eyes as I pick at the silver dress.

"You're just saying that because it's strapless." Elisa chimes in, causing Alekai to chuckle and fist bump the Maid. I hate when these two gang up on me.

"It's strapless, and I am braless. I feel like if I make one wrong move, everyone will see my body." I state, catching the possessive look in Alekai's eyes.

"No one will, and I will make sure of that!" Alekai states possessively, his eyes roaming my body with love and lust deep inside them. I roll my eyes, sighing in defeat as I motion for Alekai to lead the way. Holding his hand out to me, I gladly take it, saying goodnight to Elisa before we head out of the closet. I quickly bend down to pet Chaos and Nova, giving my pups a kiss on the head before allowing Alekai to lead me out of the room.

"So, what charity is the ball for this year?" I asked.

"It's for a women's shelter, surprisingly. Mother got to choose this year, and she chose to help a local women's shelter for abused women escaping their partners." I smile, remembering the only interaction I had with Alekai's parents and the way King Joseph groped the poor maid in front of Queen Arabess. It makes sense why she would choose this as the charity for the ball. The Queen seemed unhappy with her marriage, and I could not blame her.

"How long do we have to stay this time?" I ask, knowing that the ladies King Joseph had chosen as arranged marriage partners will be attending, including Linnate, makes me want to turn around and hide away with Alekai.

"Two hours. Then we can head back to our room and enjoy the night properly." I nod, happy to not be stuck in this dress longer than I thought. The walk ends quickly, and soon we find ourselves outside the ballroom door, the butler announcing our arrival. The first stop is to greet the King and Queen. As usual, a poor maid is at the mercy of the King while the Queen ignores the scene beside her, most likely used to it by now.

"Good evening Mother, Father." Alekai says as he bows and I curtsy. We wait for permission to rise, and when given, the Queen rises from her throne and gives me a warm hug.

"Did Alekai give you the good news?" She asks, a smile on her elegant face.

"Mother, I planned to tell her later tonight." Alekai chuckles, the Queen linking her arms in mine.

"Well, I get to tell her as she is Duke Roland's niece after all. He found Lady Jaida and Miss Aime. The problem is extracting them from their Masters." My heart stops for a moment, only for an overwhelming joy to fill me. They were alive and found, even if in a similar situation as me.

"When can we save them?" I ask, finding it fitting that this news be given at a charity ball for a women's shelter.

"Soon, I hope. Don't worry, Lyra." I nod at Alekai's words, thanking him profusely for keeping his promise to find my friends. I will be able to see them soon, and I can't wait. Queen Arabess smiles at me, handing me a handkerchief that I accept graciously and wipe a few stray tears of joy away before handing it back to her.

"Well, you two enjoy the ball. And Alekai, I won't be forcing marriage on you anymore." Saying those words, I feel her squeeze my arm before she releases me and Alekai wraps his own around my waist, giving his mother a genuine smile that I have come to know and love. Excusing herself to greet her next guests, the Queen turns to another woman whom I quickly realize is Linnate, standing by the King, the maid now gone as Linnate hands him a cup of wine from a passing waiter. Her glare is evident as she stares at me, and I smile at her as sweetly as I can before Alekai leads us away to the dancefloor, sweeping me off my feet as we twirl to the music. The room is filled with nobles and merchants, and Uncle Elyse comes to greet us after our third dance.

"Y-you found my Jaida?" His eyes water as Alekai hands him a handkerchief, my own eyes wanting to shed some tears as well.

"Yes, he did. We will be able to see her soon." I say, my voice cracking as I hug my Uncle.

"Yes, we will!" He agrees, his tear-filled eyes also filled with determination. And then we hear it.

A piercing scream rings through the ballroom, silencing the noise behind us as a hushed whisper spreads through the crowd.

"Mother!" Alekai states, turning towards the direction of the thrones before taking off, running to where the scream originated. I quickly run after him, the two of us pushing through the crowd that soon realize who was trying to get through and parting quickly, allowing a path for Alekai and I to get by. The sight that greets us has me gasping. Alekai grows pale as we stare at his mother, her hands clutching King Joseph's in hers as she begs him to wake up. Her sobbing is heart-wrenching as blood drips from the clearly dead King's mouth, nose, ears and open eyes that stare blankly into the crowd. The poor maid he was groping earlier sits frozen beside his throne with horror on her face.

"G-Guards! Lock the doors and track down any and all Palace workers and guests in the halls. No one is leaving tonight!" Alekai orders as I carefully walk towards Queen Arabess, prying her away from her dead husband and catching a weird scent that worries me as I wrap a protective arm around the weeping Queen, who promptly clings to me.

"Kai, I could be wrong, but I think this is the work of poison." I state, turning to look at him while the Queen sobs into my dress.

"I know. Only poison can do this." He agrees. Guards quickly come to our side, some pushing the crowd back, others helping to place the fallen King onto a stretcher that was wheeled in. Alekai orders them to take his body to the hospital wing, presumably for an autopsy.

"You can't take my husband from me." The Queen pleads, and my heart breaks for her as I pull her closer to me and rub her back.

"I am so sorry, but it's too late." I whisper, my own tears falling from my eyes as the heartbreak in her sobs causes me to cry. A maid quickly comes, offering to help me bring the Queen away, which I accept, letting Alekai know I will be taking her to my little kitchen, feeling that the sitting area there will be the perfect quiet place for her.

"Adam and Elisa will be there, I ordered a guard to let them know of the situation, and I will join you as soon as possible." I nod, keeping a protective arm around Queen Arabess while leading her out of the ballroom, the maid helping us up the stairs. As we reach the third step, Elisa rushes to our side, taking the place of the maid and helping me get Queen Arabess to my private room. Settling the now-widowed Queen on a sofa by the fire and wrapping a knitted throw over her shoulders. Nova jumps up beside her, letting out a soft whimper as she licks the Queen's cheek. The grieving woman turns toward the pup and cuddles her as she sobs. I pull Elisa to the side and sigh.

"Can you go to the Queen's room and grab some comfortable clothes? I'll stay with her until you come back, then slip out to change while you help her out of her gowns." I ask, running a hand through my hair, happy to only have loose curls and not an extravagant updo.

"Of course. I will be right back. Adam is just outside, so if you need anything, call for him." I nod, thanking Elisa before returning to the Queen, sitting beside her as Chaos watches from his dog bed. Elisa soon returns, and I slip out, greeting Adam, who informs me that Alekai is interrogating the guests with the guards.

I head to my bedroom, finding a set of pyjamas and leaving a comfortable set out for Alekai with a note to change before joining Queen Arabess and me. I then return to my personal room, spying Queen Arabess lying on the couch, a duvet covering her, and Nova in her arms. I thank Elisa before grabbing a book to read and curling up on the opposite couch, deciding to read while I wait for Alekai to return.

"How is she?" I look up from the book I am reading to see a dishevelled and tired-looking Alekai making his way towards me, happy to see him in the grey pyjama set I left for him. The clock behind me chimes, signalling midnight, and I yawn.

"She's been asleep for the last few hours. Nova hasn't left her side. How are you feeling?" I ask, settling my book on the side table and motioning for him to join me.

"I..." he starts as he sits beside me, but his voice cracks, and he turns to bury his face in my chest, his sobs wracking his body. I instinctively wrap my arms around him, pulling Alekai closer as he sobs, his arms wrapping around me. I know that he had a strained relationship with his Father, but King Joseph was his Father, and he was murdered in the same room as Alekai. Soon his sobs quiet down, and I realize Alekai has fallen asleep. I sigh and look outside the window, the full moon shining down on us. I pray to whatever Deity is watching over us to find the culprit and quickly heal these two grieving royals.

Chapter 23

The room is filled with quiet sobbing and the fake sounds of nobles commenting on how King Joseph will be missed. I sit between Alekai and Queen Arabess in the front pew, the Queen sobbing silently beside me as she clutches my hand. Her black veil is covering her face from the guests in the room. Alekai sits stoically like a statue, his eyes staring at the portrait of the late king on the small stage, waiting for the funeral to start.

For the last seven days, Elisa and I prepared the funeral, only inviting close friends and relatives to the viewing, all while taking care of the grieving Queen and Prince Alekai. The day after the death of King Joseph, I tried to coax the Queen into eating some chicken soup, but she vehemently refused until Elisa mentioned I worked hard to ensure the Queen stayed nourished with this meal. Upon realizing I can cook and me explaining I was a culinary student before being captured and sold, Queen Arabess finally accepted the bowl of soup, especially after seeing Alekai slowly eat his own and ask for seconds. Since then, between planning the funeral, coordinating the work of the Palace with the staff and talking with the guards about security, I took care of all the meals for the two, Queen Arabess only trusting my cooking. Every so often, she would join me in cooking, looking for a distraction, one I gladly gave her.

Finally, the Priest walks in, and we all rise, both of my hands now clutched by Alekai and the Queen as the funeral begins. The Priest begins with a sermon, talking about how God loves all his creations and how King Joseph sits in heaven with his Holiness watching over us. Queen Arabess leans into me, taking deep breaths to control her sobs as she listens to the Priest. I give her a small smile, squeezing her hand reassuringly. I notice from the corner of my eyes that Linnate is glaring at me, hatred shining in her eyes, but I pay no heed to her. Alekai and his mother need me right now. I return my focus to the

Priest, deep into another prayer. The funeral will be short and to the point, as suggested by the Queen.

"King Joseph was a wise King, one we will all remember. Let us pray for his soul, and may his reign live on..." the priest trails off, bowing his head.

"Forevermore." The crowd mumbles in unison, concluding the service. His casket is then carried away by guards, with Alekai, Queen Arabess and I following behind before the rest of the crowd as we board a carriage. A funeral procession through the city will begin, the carriage with the casket starting from the chapel and ending at the royal burial ground on the other side of the city, where the late King will be laid to rest. After a long ride and another short walk to where the casket is lowered, we say our final goodbyes to King Joseph.

I lead Alekai and his mother back to the carriages, where we are promptly driven to the Palace and ushered into the ballroom. The sombre mood of the funeral is evident as black decorates the tables, and the bright curtains adorning the windows are switched to heavy, black velvet pairs. I help Queen Arabess sit on her throne, but Alekai hesitates to sit on the one meant for the King. I encourage him since it will be his throne in a few days, after his coronation. A decorative chair is placed between the two, and I take my own seat, Elisa handing us a glass of water as the only maid trusted by the three of us right now, just as the guests arrive.

"I am so sorry..."

"Please accept my..."

"Please take your time to heal..."

The list of words said to the grieving mother and son are insincere, as few meant what they said. We all knew King Joseph was a horrible King, only helping the commoners when it suited him, but he was still our King and left behind a caring Queen who created the Charity ball to help the people. It takes everything in me not to roll my eyes when Linnate and her father step forward, expressing their deepest condolences. I watch as Linnate tries to step closer, but Adam stops her before she can even take one step, a look of annoyance flashing in her eyes.

Of course, with Linnate being banned from the Palace, only special events allow her access, and I can tell how badly she wants to worm her way closer to the Queen and Prince Alekai, but I will not allow her. Queen Arabess and I have grown closer under these unfortunate events, and she has stepped up as a mother figure these last few days, even if she is grieving. I will not allow her to be harmed, and something inside me suspects Linnate had something to do with the King's death.

The line of well-wishers finally ends with guests mingling amongst the crowd. I heave a sigh of relief, happy to be done with everyone. I smile and thank Elisa as she brings another glass of water for the three of us, the Maid standing just behind me as I take in the tired and haggard appearance of the two Royals beside me.

"Are you two ready to leave?" I ask, reaching out to squeeze Alekai's hand.

"Yes, please, all this chatter is giving me a headache." Queen Arabess agrees quickly, Alekai and I standing to help his mother to her feet and lead her out of the ballroom, with Adam and Elisa trailing behind us. Guards patrol the halls, nodding at us respectfully as we navigate the quiet corridors to the stairs, where we make our ascent to my little kitchen.

"Have the two of you eaten anything today?" I ask once Arabess settles into a sofa. Nova and Chaos instantly bound onto the seat beside her and snuggle into the woman.

"I had something small," Queen Arabess answers.

"Not since yesterday." I frown at Alekai, sighing as I lean down and kiss his cheek while he leans into the armchair by the fire.

"I'll make something simple then." With that, I quickly get to work on a simple lunch of baked chicken and salad with raspberry vinaigrette, serving a plate to Arabess and Alekai as Elisa dismisses herself to other work. I keep an eye on the Queen, watching her tired face light up as she enjoys her meal and plays with the pups, happy to see some form of emotion other than sadness and despair on her face.

"If you'd like, I let Elisa and Adam watch the pups normally, but I can leave the two with you on days Alekai and I need some alone time." I suggest, seeing Queen Arabess' face light up.

"I'd love that."

"How about Lyra also teaches you how to bake and cook as well?" Alekai suggests, giving me a smile. I agree instantly, mentioning some treats Queen Arabess likes to eat that she can learn to bake.

"I will only agree to have you teach me on one condition." Queen Arabess states, a stern look on her face.

"What is your condition?" I ask perplexed and worried.

"Call me Ara or Mother," She smiles at me warmly, and I look at her in shock, turning to Alekai, who gives me a small nod of encouragement. I quickly leap to my feet, walking to Arabess and sitting beside her, taking her hand in mine.

"I can't promise to call you Mother just yet, but I can call you Ara and Arabess if that is okay," I state, feeling as if calling someone Mother is strange as I had lost mine young. A look of understanding crosses Arabess' face before she pulls me into a hug, tears welling in my eyes at the motherly affection she is giving me.

"I can accept that. But one day, you'll call me Mother. I just know it." She whispers, and I nod as I hug her back. With a new understanding between Arabess and I, the two of us make the short walk to the kitchen where we spend the day baking. Alekai watches from the sidelines while Elisa brings some work for him to complete. I feel content, like I belong with these two as a family.

Chapter 24

The soft, fall breeze ruffles through my hair as I watch Alekai running around with Nova and Chaos. Elisa hands cups of hot tea to Arabess and I while we enjoy the warm sun. The two of us are poring over a binder, going over the plans for Alekai's coronation that will be taking place in a few days. I sigh, realizing just how big of an event this will be while having the responsibility of planning such an event for the last three weeks.

But a Kingdom cannot go without a leader for too long.

"Lyra, be honest with me." Arabess starts, taking the binder from my hand and placing it on the chair beside her.

"Aren't I always?" I retort, stretching to reach the plate of cookies in the middle of the table.

"Alekai doesn't want to marry Linnate, does he?" I nearly choke on a bite of a chocolate chip cookie, quickly taking a sip of my tea to help the dessert down my throat before turning to look at Arabess incredulously.

"He despises her. Trust me when I say that if there were any small reason to imprison her in the dungeons, she would be chained down there." I answer honestly, seeing Arabess chuckle.

"I had a feeling that may be the case. You see, Joseph wanted a strong alliance with many Nobles and Royals around the world by using his children. But, because of complications while giving birth, Alekai is the only child we were able to have. Truth be told, I find that little hussy a horrible fit as Queen." I watch as disgust crosses her face and relief fills me, happy to know that Arabess did not approve of Linnate at all.

"So, why did you argue with Alekai to marry her?" I ask, taking her hand in mine. I have been wondering about it for a while, especially when Alekai would leave me alone to have his meetings with his parents.

"Because that's what Joseph wanted. No matter what, I couldn't say no to the King. He made sure I learned that long ago." A lone tear falls down the aging woman's face, and my heart breaks for her. Wrapping my arms around Arabess, I reassure her that her life can only get better from here, that she still could find love at forty-one years old.

"One-day, Alekai will tell us who he wishes to marry as his Queen, and I have a feeling that day will be soon." Arabess whispers as we pull away, a knowing smile on her face that leaves me slightly confused. She returns the binder to the table between us, taking out a list that I recognize is the food for the ball that will take place after the coronation. She hands it to me, asking for my opinion. Everything looks perfect, and I hand it to the personal maid of Arabess, asking her to bring the list to Ali.

I turn to see Arabess looking at me with emotion I can't decipher. Arabess learned quickly that I could not continue to be her personal chef eight days after the funeral, and I took the opportunity to introduce the Queen to Ali and her team. After a few tests and another week of the food being tested secretly, Arabess appointed Ali and the others as the royal family's personal chef and the head chef for special events.

Ali could not stop thanking me for days, sending new deserts and scrumptious meals to my room every chance she could, along with recipes she created herself. At one point, I had to scold my friend and explain that she had earned this opportunity and no longer needed to thank me.

With the food decided on, I ask Arabess to double-check the guest list. I would need her expertise as Queen for the last twenty-seven years in this decision.

"Viscount Raylack and his wife will not be able to attend; they are on vacation. Lord and Lady Mirrose will be late by an hour, thinking they are better than others, so remove them and their family from the coronation guest list." She continues to cross off names from the list, removing twenty people. I nod, taking in the information of the guests she excluded and making a note in the binder for future reference. I have a feeling I will be helping these two host balls and banquets in the future, and knowing who to exclude will be helpful.

With the list now set, I smile and take out the invitation sample agreed upon yesterday from the binder, turning to Elisa, who waits patiently behind me.

"Elisa, please take these to the calligraphers and have them create and send these invitations out to the guests."

"Of course, Miss Lyra," Elisa replies, smiling at me as she scurries off to fulfill the task.

"You really sound like a Royal, bossing around the servants like this." Alekai chuckles, bending down to plant a kiss on my temple before giving his mother a hug.

"Well, someone has to make sure your special day goes smoothly." I chuckle, watching him take a pastry from the table and devour it in two bites. Arabess shoots a disapproving look at her son, handing him a napkin before turning to me.

"Just be glad I raised him and not his father." She jokingly states, causing her son to roll his eyes.

"Well, Mother, I am glad you raised me because I am a one-woman type of man." Alekai states, sitting beside me and taking my hand, placing a gentle kiss on top of my knuckles. I blush, his words causing butterfly flutters inside me.

"Why don't you and Lyra go out for the night? Chaos and Nova will be fine with me, and you two can get away from the Palace." I see Arabess give Alekai a look as if the two are hiding a secret from me, causing me to be curious. I give them both a questioning look, but instead of prying, I return my focus to the coronation planning until the binder is taken away, and Alekai looks at me with an amused smile.

"Lyra, you've worked hard enough." Arabess mock scolds me, accepting the binder from her son and placing it out of reach.

"I know, but I just want everything to be perfect." I agree, running my fingers through my hair.

"With you and Mother planning it, the coronation will be amazing. Now come, I have something planned for us." Alekai cuts in, standing and holding his hand out for me. I sigh, placing my hand in his as Elisa and Margarite—Arabess' maid—return after fulfilling their tasks.

"Leaving already?" Elisa asks.

"Yes, is everything set?" Alekai answers, smiling at Elisa as she gives me a knowing look.

"Yes, Your Highness. Nick is out front with the limousine." Elisa smiles, turning to give me a hug and whispering congratulations, confusing me even more before Alekai shoos her away and leads me out of his study. Trying to pry information out of Alekai, I cuddle close to his side, trying to be coy to see if he would tell me what is going on. Still, he just chuckles and whispers you'll see in my ear when we exit the Palace and enter the limousine I haven't seen since being brought to the Palace almost three months ago.

Chapter 25

I watch the streets pass as the limousine heads to the northeastern side of town. Although Lotross is the capital of Symphrain, it is located in the northern part of a province once known as Ontario, back when this part of the continent was Canada. A memory surfaces to mind, the one where my history teacher taught us how the Kingdom of Symphrain came to be.

As children, we are taught that the northernmost part of the country and its provinces were spared from World War Three due to the low population. But after the war-torn country crumbled, the Nightwood family took charge in helping those in need of food and stability make their way to Symphrain, where the wealthy family's manor stood. Slowly it grew into a large city, the Palace being built two hours away from the original manor where a city soon started. And as the population grew with technological advances taking place and the lands once destroyed by bombs became fertile again, more towns and cities appeared. Thus Symphrain was renamed Lotross, and the Nightwood family renamed the country Canada to the Kingdom of Symphrain.

"Alekai, how long will it take us to reach where we are going?" I ask, turning to face him and leaning into his body.

"About two hours." He answers, wrapping his arms around me and pulling me closer, his hands running through my hair. I have a hunch about where this limousine is taking us. The memory reminds me that the original manor was located by a secluded lake about north to northeast of the city, and only the royal family and their relatives could enter the well-guarded area. But I still wanted to be sure where we were going.

"Are you going to tell me where we are going?" I ask, nuzzling his jaw and trailing kisses, hoping my charm can break his calm façade.

"Do you really want to know?" He chuckles, moving quickly and maneuvering us to where I find myself on my back with him on top of me, kneeling between my legs.

"Yes," I whisper, my breath hitching as he leans forward, trailing kisses from my collarbone, up my neck and ending beside my ear, his heavy breathing causing my body to react as my lower abdomen starts to feel heavy with need.

"Well, Songbird, it's a surprise." Alekai chuckles in my ear, biting the sensitive lobe before turning to capture my lips with a dominating kiss. His tongue delves into mine, and I submit, wrapping my legs around his waist as I grind into him, feeling the hard bulge through the fabric of our clothing.

The kiss ends, leaving me gasping for breath, but he doesn't stop there. His lips trail down my neck and over the swell of my breasts, where one hand pulls my shirt down, leaving my breasts on display for Alekai to do as he sees fit. His lips quickly find my perked nipple, sucking the hard bud into his mouth as he swirls his tongue around it, teasing the small bud and making me moan loudly as the ache between my legs grows. Breast milk begins to flow, and Alekai drinks his fill while his free hand trails down my stomach and pushes the skirt and thong I wear aside. His fingers find my soaking wet pussy, teasing the entrance with slow circles. His lips switch from the now thoroughly abused nipple to the neglected one, once again teasing and suckling from me while one finger slips inside, another lewd moan being coaxed out of me.

"What's wrong, Lyra?" he asks, slightly condescending.

"I... I want you." My voice is a needy whimper, surprising even myself at how wanton I sound.

"Aw, why's that, Little Songbird?" He continues, slipping another finger inside me.

"B... Because I am horny." I admit, my face flushing in embarrassment. Alekai chuckles, his lips descending onto mine as he claims me in a kiss, his tongue dancing with mine as I taste the creaminess of my breast milk on his lips. I find myself grinding against his fingers, moaning into the kiss as my body heats, aching to feel Alekai deep inside me, filling me. But he pulls away, his fingers slowly working their magic inside me as he watches me, moaning and begging for him to fill me.

"Not yet, Lyra." He chuckles, his fingers speeding up. I feel my walls twitch, my thighs growing wet with my juices as I try to find release, but he taunts me, pulling his fingers out and only rubbing the entrance to my pussy. Too wrapped up in the pleasure, my mind a haze of need and wanting to be filled, I fail to notice the car stop or that I have been moved inside wherever we arrived. I find myself on a large bed naked and on my hands and knees with Alekai behind me, keeping me from falling onto the soft mattress while his tongue slides across my dripping pussy, diving deep inside me. I scream his name as he feasts on my cum, my walls finally having enough of his torture while I cum. I hear a deep chuckle, my body wanting to fall onto the bed, but his hands hold my hips, making me stay on my hands and knees as he positions himself behind me, rubbing the tip of his hard cock against me.

"Please." I whimper, turning to look back at him.

"Please, what, Lyra?" Alekai asks, slowly inserting the tip before pulling out, my body shivering.

"Please fill me."

"With pleasure, Songbird." With that Alekai thrusts hard inside me, forcing a long moan out of my throat as he groans with pleasure. He takes me from behind, fingers digging into me as I try to match his speed, my body moulding like clay in his hands. I want to curse the serums, but the pleasure reminds me that I belong to the man who holds my body close to his from behind, his lips kissing and biting my skin as he moans my name.

He abruptly pulls out of me, manipulating my jelly-like body onto my back before thrusting inside once more, my body trembling as I cum again, feeling Alekai stiffen above me before the unmistakable heat of his seed releasing inside me brings my pleasure high down. He presses his body weight on me, wrapping his arms around my body and rolling us over, with me resting on top of him and his cock still deep inside me, twitching.

Our breaths are ragged, the intensity of our lovemaking different from before. And then I feel it.

The chain I was used to being around my neck slides off. My neck feels lighter as Alekai removes the chain from where it fell on his body and places it on the side table, just within reach.

"Why?" I ask, looking up at Alekai.

"Because I love you. I want the woman I love to rule beside me as an equal, not as someone I own." He answers, hugging me closer to his body.

"You love me?" I ask in a whisper, my voice cracking as I try to keep the tears from falling.

"I love you, Lyra." He answers warmly, placing a soft kiss on my forehead. I lose the fight as tears flow happily down my face, and I bury my face in the crook of his neck. My heart feels light as I realize what I have been fighting for the last few weeks.

"I love you too, Alekai."

Chapter 26

Soft fingers slowly drawing circles on my back wake me from my sleep, from the dream of Alekai and I confessing our love for each other and him setting me free as his slave. It was a great dream, but reality crashed around me as soon as I opened my eyes. I sigh, snuggling closer to the warm body, a deep chuckle filling my ears.

"Good morning Lyra." Alekai's voice calls out gently, a kiss placed on my temple.

"Morning, Kai." I yawn, opening my eyes to see a gentle smile on his face. My hand moves to adjust the necklace on my neck, feeling nothing but my skin under my fingertips instead. I jolt upright, realizing we were not in our usual room as I look around, spotting the chain I grew accustomed to around my neck sitting on the nightstand beside the bed.

"It wasn't a dream?" I ask, tears forming in my eyes.

"It wasn't a dream, Lyra. You're free." Alekai proclaims, sitting up beside me and pulling me into his lap. I cry, realizing my blissful dream is reality. Alekai and I are in love with each other, and I no longer have the status of a sex slave. Alekai just holds me, allowing me to cry my heart out as the emotions of finally being his equal and finding someone who loves me unconditionally run their course until I am left breathless, leaning against the man I love.

"You okay, beautiful?" He asks, wiping stray tears from my cheeks.

"I am." I answer, meaning it with every fibre of my being. I am loved by a man who has shown he cares about me time and time again after our rough start. We lay in bed, Alekai cuddling me close to his body as we just talk. I learn that Alekai was a troublemaker as a child, and he tells the story of him filling the fountain with dish soap from the kitchen until bubbles filled the garden, causing me to laugh until my sides hurt.

"You were a menace. I hope any children we have aren't like you." I giggle, my statement gaining me an eye roll.

"Well, what was your childhood like?" He rebuts, and I frown.

"Not one I want to relive." I whisper quietly, taking a deep breath as I recount the abuse my father threw my way before I was accepted into boarding school. My decision to become a baker was based on countless nights of going to bed hungry because women and booze were more important to the man who was supposed to raise me.

"The reason Jaida and Aime are so important to me is because those two saved me. I was the poor scholarship girl with no money for luxuries. They became my friends, then sisters, and their parents became family to me." I end with, Alekai once again drawing soothing circles on my skin.

"Well, I will be your family now, and you will never go hungry again. That's a promise." His words reassure me as I know that Alekai will keep this promise. The thought of living with him in the Palace for the rest of our lives and continuing to get to know the man who holds me securely in his arms is something I look forward to waking up to every day.

"Can we change the subject?" I ask.

"Sure, anything you want to talk about?"

"Yes, why did you bring me to the Manor? The one where your family first started to rule?" I look up to see Alekai staring at me in shock and surprise but also a hint of pride and amazement. I guess he never thought I would figure out where we are.

"You never cease to amaze me, Songbird," He whispers incredulously, planting a swift kiss on my lips.

"Answer the question, mister." I mock scold, gaining a chuckle.

"Okay, okay. There is the tradition that before a Prince takes the throne, he brings the woman he wishes to be his Queen here to confess their love and, well, enjoy some adult fun like we did last night." I blush at the mention of our lovemaking, realizing I was like an animal in heat.

"So this means I will be Queen?" I ask.

"Of course. Why do you think Mother has been having you help her with planning the coronation? She is seeing just how capable you are. I also told her you're the one that came up with names for my school and the idea of training farmers. She already approves of you as her replacement." I never thought I could burst with happiness but his words and knowing that Arabess approves of me cause more tears to flow. Alekai allows me to cry once more, and I apologize, not being one to cry easily. I feel embarrassed, but he holds me tighter, reassuring me that his shoulder will always be for me to cry, sleep, and lean on.

Our stay in the Manor is short. Alekai shows me the rich history of where Symphrain first began and takes me swimming in the lake. The gardens have become my favourite place to sit, eat, and stroll with Alekai, talking about everything and nothing. Three days later and feeling very refreshed after a long time, Nick arrives in the limousine, and we soon drive away from the fairytale-like place.

"Will we be able to visit here again?" I ask, watching the trees of the dense forest pass by.

"Of course, Lyra. Just let me know when and I will make sure to have one full week for us to relax here." Alekai assures me, pressing a kiss to my temple before turning to focus on the file Elisa sent for Alekai to review before we return home.

Chapter 27

I smile as I listen to Alekai speak to Uncle Elyse about the school's success, his soothing voice filled with excitement at the future prospect this trades school will bring to Symphrain.

"Yes, she's right here." He chuckles, holding out the phone to me, which I gladly accept.

"Hi, Uncle Elyse." I greet him right away and lean into Alekai, who plants a kiss on top of my head.

"Lyra, congratulations. Arabess already told me Alekai's plans, and I must say, you as Queen is an amazing idea." I blush at his praise, looking at Alekai with a raised brow. He just smiles back, turning to look out the window while I return to the phone call.

"Thank you. I know it will be a lot of work, but I am up for the challenge." Uncle Elyse chuckles at this.

"I also have word on Jaida and Aime. Jaida actually called me yesterday. She will be returning home within the week. Aime has actually been in the city, but that's all I know." My eyes widen at the news, and I quickly ask about their well-being, feeling relieved to hear my friends are healthy. Of course, like me, Jaida and Aime were sold as slaves, but knowing Jaida regained her freedom and will be home safe is news I have been waiting for. Unfortunately, not knowing more about Aime has my feelings conflicted with both happiness and sadness. I will be able to see Jaida soon, but Aime will be a different story.

"Will Jaida be attending the coronation?" I ask, going to reach for the necklace that normally hung around my neck to fiddle with, only to remember it is gone.

"I am not sure. Sorry, Lyra." Uncle Elyse answers, a sigh escaping his lips.

"That's fine. I am simply happy she will be home safe." Our conversation turns to one about the school, with Uncle Elyse asking me to meet before the coronation and come for a tour of the school after the coronation, to which

I agree excitedly before hanging up. Passing the phone to Alekai, I yawn, my body exhausted from recent events.

"Why don't you sleep?" Alekai whispers, pulling me onto his lap and resting my head on his shoulder, one hand cradling my head while playing with my hair, the other keeping me close. I yawn again, unable to respond before closing my eyes, sleep taking over quickly.

∞

"Welcome home, Your –"

"Shhhh, Lyra is asleep. I think she's been working too hard lately." Alekai's voice is a whisper, seeping into my dreams as he quiets whoever is greeting him. I open my eyes slightly, seeing the familiar halls of the Palace through my sleep-filled eyes.

"Kai?" I croak out, turning my face into his shoulder to block out the hallway lights.

"Don't worry, Lyra, go back to sleep. I'll wake you when food is ready." His low voice soothes me, and I nod slightly, closing my eyes and breathing in the usual scent of roses and mint from the bathing set he always uses, the comforting scent lulling me gently to sleep. I feel my body lowering into a bed, Alekai's scent mixing with my usual vanilla scent, letting me know I am safe and sound in our room.

"Sweet dreams, my Songbird." Alekai whispers, kissing my forehead. I smile, feeling his hand run through my hair as sleep begins to take hold of me. Before once again slipping into dreamland, I feel something being placed around my neck, a comforting weight solidifying the sense of security I feel as I fall asleep again.

Chapter 28

"Is she awake, My Lady?" A voice calls out, and the harsh light of the room is turned on, waking me from my sleep to full alertness as I bolt awake.

"Shut up, you moron." A familiar voice seethes. I frown, instantly going on alert while trying to find the emergency button normally kept by my bedside table.

"But for your information, I watched as Prince Alekai carried the whore into the Palace while Father and I pleaded our case to be able to enter freely." My hand touches a folded piece of paper in the dark. Not wanting Linnate to find it, I carefully slip it into my pocket, slowly sliding towards Alekai's side of the bed in hopes of escaping from the room and locking myself in the closet. At least from there, I can slip into the hidden staircase and run to the study, where I can either find Alekai working or call for the guards. Before I can slip off the bed, the lights are switched on, causing me to hiss as I close my eyes from the sudden change. Forcing my eyes open after cursing at myself for my reaction, I come face to face with Linnate, who stands before me, a smirk on her smug face.

"Hello, Bitch." She sneers, glaring at me as I look at her appearance. A simple pastel pink dress hangs off her body, giving the appearance of an innocent young woman, but I knew better.

"Shouldn't I be the one calling you that?" I ask, getting into a sitting position while looking at the angry-looking female. This remark earns me a hard slap across the face, my head being forced to the right from the momentum while my left cheek stings from the contact. I glare at her, refusing to look weak in front of this mentally unstable person.

"That is no way to speak to your future Queen." Linnate huffs, and I chuckle, getting on my feet and pushing the woman away from me, watching her stumble to regain her balance.

130

"Again, Linnate, shouldn't I be the one saying that!" I retort, crossing my arms over my chest while trying to for her back enough so I can run to safety. She screams in anger, her arm raised once again to hit me, but her accomplice holds her back, the man glaring at me as well.

"My Lady, you can't hit her. Her necklace is recording still." The mysterious man warns, and my smirk grows. I noticed earlier a familiar weight around my neck, realizing Alekai had placed another necklace on me. I pray that it is the original necklace, hoping that whatever Linnate has planned for me will be foiled with the safety this necklace brings.

"You're right, drug her, and let's finish what we came for." Linnate easily agrees, surprisingly. But I am already climbing back over the bed, Linnate screaming for the man to grab me as I take whatever I can grab and throw it at him. Vases, pillows, books, and anything I can reach are thrown at Linnate and her accomplice as I run towards the closet, knowing that once I get inside, I have a chance to escape these two. But something hits me in the back, causing me to trip and fall onto the floor, where Linnate's accomplice quickly holds me down. I feel a prick on my neck and something being injected into me, whatever drug quickly taking effect as my body becomes weak and my vision blurry.

"My Lady, please ensure the coast is clear so we can leave." The man requests, releasing me from his hold. The door to the bedroom opens, and I try to think of a way to leave a message, spotting a red lipstick just in reach. Elisa will kill me for this, but I struggle until the lipstick cap is off and look for something to write on, spying a book that must have ended up under the table beside me. With the little strength I have left, I use the lipstick and write one message before my consciousness slips away – SAVE ME!

Chapter 29

My eyes slowly open to the dripping sound of water hitting the floor nearby. My head feels like a brick has been thrown at it, while my body feels weighed down. I sigh, slowly taking in my surroundings, noticing the small dingy room with an equally dirty sink where the water drips into and a semi-clean small toilet I realize I will have to use eventually. Then, turning to the right, I see the wall in front is made of thick bars. This is a prison, and I am an unwilling prisoner. My thoughts turn to try to figure out how I can free myself, the thin cot I lay on not providing any comfort or luxury that I had grown used to. The prison I lay in reminds me of the dark days when my father would lock me in the basement while he attended to his current fling. I want out, I want Alekai and his comfort.

"Look who is finally up!" A shrill voice calls out, and I bolt into a sitting position, instantly regretting the quick change of position as I rush to the toilet, where any remaining food in my stomach is quickly emptied into the bowl. I want to groan, my head pounding and stomach churning, but showing any more weakness in front of this hell spawn is not an option.

"Aw, poor Little Songbird, running away from her Prince that loves her so much after regaining her freedom." Linnate taunts, leaning against the wall opposite my cell.

"Do you have proof that's what Alekai believes?" I ask, feeling confident that my man knows the truth.

"It's all over the Palace, how the Prince returned to his room to find it empty with a note from you left behind." She chuckles. I roll my eyes, remembering the mess the room was left in and knowing Alekai, he made a rumour in order to fish out the person who kidnapped me. Poor Linnate only has a few days before being caught with how loyal and diligent Alekai is.

"So, Linnate, enlighten me as to why you are doing all of this." I suggest, standing up from the floor and pushing my hair out of my face. I watch as she thinks about this idea, slowly returning to the thin bed and sitting on the edge. "That's not a bad idea, but it's a long one, so let me get a chair." I chuckle softly as this spoiled bitch walks away, shoving my hands in the pocket of my pants I feel something push against my fingertips and freeze, remembering the piece of paper I shoved in there while trying to sneak away from Linnate and her lackey. Taking a moment to listen for her arrival, I quickly take out the paper, feeling bad seeing how crumpled it is. Unfolding the paper, careful not to rip it, tears well in my eyes as I read the note

Lyra,

I know how weird it has been for you to become my pet and now be the love of my life. I also know that the weight of the necklace became something so familiar in your everyday life that I bought a replica for you.

The replica only has my Crest and a function where everything around you is recorded with audio and visual. You can take it off whenever you want because I trust you. I want you to be free, Songbird, and know that I am hopelessly in love with you and will always be here waiting for you.

Always yours,

Alekai

I sit there, fighting back the tears as I carefully fold the note and place it in my pocket again. My hand goes to the necklace, caressing it gently as I think about the man who has stolen my heart, wondering if he and Arabess are closer to finding me now. The sounds of footsteps alert me to Linnate's return, and I sit up, wiping my eyes dry and turning towards the cell door . Linnate greets me with what I assume is a triumphant smile on her punchable face as her lackey sets a padded chair in front of the cell bars but out of reach from me possibly grabbing and hurting this bitch. Remembering the function of this new necklace, I position the charm and my body and pray that Linnate and her accomplice are in full view. When I ever get free, Alekai can use this as evidence. "So you want to know why I did this?" Linnate asks smugly, leaning against the chair nonchalantly while I roll my eyes.

"No, I asked because I was bored." I state sarcastically, seeing her jaw clench at my words.

"Either way, you are a dead woman, so I might as well tell you," Linnate states, taking a deep breath.

"It all started three years ago when I first debuted at the spring Charity ball. There I fell for Alekai the first time I saw him, but he never paid attention to me. So I tried everything that night to get a chance to dance with him, show him myself and hope he would fall in love with me. But that oblivious fool only had eyes for a business contract with Duke Roland and a few other men." She begins, and I chuckle. This seems like an Alekai thing, if I heard any.

"But someone did take notice of me, King Joseph. He summoned me to his office a week after the ball, and I was scared, thinking I had done something wrong. Instead, he praised me for my beauty and skills in dancing. A maid stood beside him the whole time, and then he asked if I was a virgin." Her smile becomes soft, and I frown, remembering that noblewomen debut when they turn eighteen at the Charity Ball following their birthday. I have a feeling about where this story will go, and my heart aches for Linnate.

"Of course, I answered him honestly, and he asked if I wanted to know what a man could do for her. At first, I refused, and the King agreed that I was too young and could wait. So we spent time talking and getting to know each other. For months I would walk into his office, the King shooing away the current maid by his side as we talked, and I soon fell in love with him. One day after a year of talking, he confessed how unhappy he was without any children other than Prince Alekai, and I instantly suggested I carry his children. The next thing I knew, I was under him as he took my virginity and made me a full woman. I became addicted to him, always finding ways to spend alone time with Joseph, allowing him to do everything he ever wanted to me and loving as he filled him with his cock and cum." I fake gag, cutting off her story and roll my eyes.

"So he groomed you into being his breeding vessel." I point out, getting a scoff in return.

"No, he loved me! If anything, he wasn't supposed to die, Arabess was!" She shouts in anger, her words shocking me.

"Now shut up and let me talk!" I raise my hands in surrender, deciding to allow this spoiled brat to finish her story as it will become compelling evidence against her.

"Anyway, after two years of meeting in secrecy, Joseph admitted he would love to make me his Queen but couldn't because of that bitch of a wife. So instead, he suggested I marry Alekai. Of course, any child of mine would be tested to see if Joseph is the father as we would continue our affair behind the mother and son's back, and the child that was his would be the next Crown Prince after Alekai became King. But I asked what would happen if the Queen were to pass away. He said that after a year of mourning, he would personally marry me. As you can figure out, I was ecstatic and placed into motion a plan to kill her. But unfortunately, the maid made a mistake and gave the King the wrong cup. I was upset as I had just finished telling Joseph I was pregnant with his child, excited for us to be parents. But then he passed from the poison."

"So you were attempting to kill Mother but instead killed her husband?" I ask, cutting Linnate off again.

"You call her Mother?" Linnate asks in disbelief, and I freeze, realizing that I had indeed just said that. Arabess became a mother figure to me over the weeks and knowing that the real target with not the dead King but the woman who has bonded with me causes me to want to kill the culprit and protect the woman who means so much to Alekai and I.

"You know what, that isn't important. To answer, yes, Arabess was supposed to die. I would have married Joseph and had our child as the next Queen. But now, I have to convince Prince Alekai to marry and fuck me in order to play off the child inside me as his own." She smiles, rubbing her flat stomach as something inside me breaks. To think this woman wanted to pose Alekai's unborn brother as his son is sickening.

"But there seems to be a snag with you, Lyra. You are actually pregnant as well." Linnate states, slamming a fist into the arm of the chair and shocking me. Pregnant. Me. This would explain the mood swings and my body's unexpected reactions.

"So, what are you going to do with me?" I ask, placing a protective hand over my flat stomach.

"For now, I will keep you alive until after the coronation in two days. Then, I will have you killed as if an accident happened." With that, Linnate leaves me to my thoughts as I think about not only my well-being but also that of the unborn child inside me. Alekai and I had created life, a baby of our own, and escaping this cell and returning to Alekai's side is something I have to succeed in as soon as possible.

Chapter 30

I sit on the cold cot pressed against the wall while protectively covering my stomach. It's been a day since waking up locked in the cell with no food or water. I worry for the unborn baby inside me, knowing I will need to eat soon for both of our sakes. I think about how weeks ago, I wanted to leave this Palace and regain my freedom as a citizen, and now I want to leave this cell to protect my home, my friends inside it, and the family I have with Alekai and Arabess.

The crisp sounds of heels clacking alert me to my visitor, the one bitch I want to kill. But I sigh, knowing that the baby inside her is also innocent. She can die after birthing the little royal, as I am positive Arabess would love to play it off as her own with the King as a miracle baby if the idea is suggested to her. Soon Linnate is standing at the door to the cell, her smug look just needing a good slap to wipe it off her face.

"Hello, Bitch." She calls out, and I chuckle.

"Linnate, we've been through this. Shouldn't I be calling you that?" I ask, looking defiantly at my captor.

"Don't be so smug. I am only here to tell you that fucking Joseph lied to me. He did have an arranged marriage contract ready to be signed, but Alekai never signed it, and I won't be Queen. Keeping you alive won't matter anymore as I plan to kill you after the coronation tomorrow." I chuckle, happy to know that Alekai defied his father at every turn, remembering how the contract had been snuck into his work to sign but promptly shredded before a pen could ever touch the dotted line. It seems like even forging the signature did not work either, as Alekai has a specific way he does it.

"Why don't you just find some other Noble to force into being the baby's father?" I ask, enjoying her temper tantrum. I watch as she takes the cushioned chair she sat on yesterday and throws it against the wall, breaking the front legs off it. Her lackey stands to the side, eyes shifting between us with worry.

136

"I refuse to marry just anyone. I will be Queen." She growls after a moment, chest heaving for air. I once more roll my eyes at her, getting comfortable in my spot, only for my stomach to growl loudly.

"Is someone hungry?" Linnate asks tauntingly.

"Nope." I lie, but my stomach protests again, and I frown. I am starving to be honest.

"Oh well, hopefully starving you will cause your death faster." She chuckles before leaving with her lackey, their footsteps echoing down the hall. I sigh, closing my eyes in hopes of preserving as much energy as possible while waiting for a chance to escape.

"Are... Are you hungry, Miss?" A small voice calls out sometime later, and I look to see the lackey standing by the door, eyes darting about as if watching for someone.

"Why would I take anything from you?! You helped that bitch abduct me!" I state, letting my anger seep out. I watch as the man flinches, a look of guilt taking over his features. Interesting.

"Truth be told Ma'am, I was the cleaner for the King's room. I watched the affair and was sworn to secrecy or risk my only daughter being taken as the King's slave like you." The man starts, placing the tray down under the bars and sliding it towards me.

"I thought that with his death, I could leave this Palace and protect my poor daughter, but Linnate captured her. She has been holding my poor Alice captive for the last month, threatening to kill her if I don't help." I watch tears slowly fall down his face, my heart breaking for this man. He had no say in helping the King and Linnate. Everything he has done was to protect his child, and as a mother-to-be myself, I can empathize with him.

"Will Linnate release your daughter?" I ask, scooting forward and taking in the man's appearance.

"Yes, tomorrow before the coronation. She plans to poison you and have me bring your body out and throw you into a pond." I nod, accepting his information while looking at the food on the ground.

"When will she poison me?" I ask, debating on eating the offered food or not.

"She will bring you a bottle of water with the poison inside it. What she does not know is I have switched the bottles already. I don't want you to die. I need your help in getting my Alice back and bringing this bitch to her death." He answers, and I believe him. This man has been seen around the Palace before, always loyal to the King and sometimes helping Arabess when needed.

"So, what do I do?" I see a look of relief on his face as the man collapses onto the ground, a sigh escaping his lips.

"As stated, I have switched the bottles out. All you need to do is drink the contents and react as if you can't breathe. From there, Linnate will want me to verify that you are dead, and I will. Knowing that conceited bitch, she will bring Alice with her to witness the murder and hold it above my head." He pauses, and I wait, allowing the man some time to think his words carefully.

"She will leave for the coronation, leaving Alice and I to clean up. From there, we can help you to the coronation and set you free. I know that chain is a fake, but Linnate doesn't. That's why we are in the Palace catacombs. So that the function of alerting the guards to your position doesn't go off."

"How do you know this is a fake?" I ask.

"Because I am the one who made these collars for the Royals. Prince Alekai asked for this specific necklace for you." I smile, feeling that Linnate's days are numbered.

"So basically, I pretend to be dead in order to expose this bitch." I summarize, seeing his face light up.

"Yes." I nod, looking towards the food and questioning if I can eat it.

"I swear it's safe, I assume that the babe inside you is the Prince's, and the thought of killing an innocent child is something I do not want to live with." I wait for a moment before getting up and picking up the tray of food. The smell of chicken noodle soup and fresh bread causes my stomach to growl again. There is even a bottle of cold water beside the bowl of soup, the condensation exciting me as I slide back on the hard cot and dig into my meal. I learn the lackey's name is Alister, a simple man who lost his wife to cancer three years ago when his daughter was twelve. He never remarried, instead devoting his time to raising Alice and working so she could go to a good school and make something of her life.

"So she wants to be a farmer?" I ask, shocked at this news.

"Yes, my Alice loves working with her hands and even has a garden in our backyard. I wanted her to do more but accepted that a farming life suits her the most." I smile and explain to Alister the school Alekai and Uncle Elyse opened up, that after I am free, I will put in a good word to get Alice into the farming program as long as I am alive and safe. This suggestion solidifies our alliance against Linnate, and with the food done and Alister needing to go back to work, I lay in the bed happily, a plan set in motion to return to Alekai and give Linnate her destruction.

Chapter 31

I sit leaning against the wall, head tilted back as I massage my temples, cursing the sounds of the trumpets that reach even the cells of the catacombs. The migraine is torturing me even more than the chilly, damp air. Today is coronation day, and my heart breaks at the thought of not watching as Alekai becomes King, of not standing beside his mother at the bottom of the stage while the Priest places a crown on top of his head. Instead, the two will be facing today alone, all the plans made by Arabess and I now on her shoulders to make sure today goes perfectly while I wait for the plan to start and escape from this cell. Three distinct sounds of footsteps draw near, and I smirk. It's show time.

"Oh, Lyra!" Linnate calls out, slamming something against the metal bars of the cell. I open my eyes, turning to look at the bitch wearing a light pink ball gown, her hair piled high on top of her head, revealing her slender neck and intricate jewelry.

"What do you want, Linnate?" I ask quietly, taking in the third person of the group with her hands tied in front of her. The girl appears to be in her teens, her dress dishevelled and dirty and her hair a tangled mess around her scarred and bruised face. A black collar is wrapped around her neck, a lead clipped to it where the line ends in Linnate's right hand. This must be Alice.

"I want you to do me a favour. Drink this bottle, or this pretty little girl will die. She is, after all, Alekai's half-sister." Linnate states, holding out a bottle in front of her as she smiles smugly at me. My eyes widen in mock surprise, already ready for the lies this woman will spew from her mouth thanks to Alister's information last night.

"How do I know you aren't lying?" I ask, getting off the cot and pushing myself against the cell bars, reaching out for Linnate who promptly steps back. Alister steps in, standing between the bars and Linnate like we planned and reaches into a bag where he promptly takes out a document for me to read.

"As you can see here, this young lady is indeed King Joseph's daughter." He states, winking at me, our cue that the drink is indeed safe for me to consume. I pretend to slump in defeat at the fake document, taking a deep breath.

"What's in the bottle, Linnate?" I ask, glaring at the bottle in her left hand that she promptly hands to Alister.

"Nothing really, just a nice drink that will eliminate you."

"So, poison." She chuckles and tugs on the lead, pulling Alice forward as the poor girl stumbles over.

"So what's your choice, you and the baby or the Princess beside me?" Linnate asks, and I sigh in defeat, reaching through the bars and accepting the drink from Alistar.

"If I drink this, will you let the girl go?" I ask.

"Of course. I may be heartless, but this girl is my ticket to becoming Queen." I nod, looking at the girl and giving her a soft smile before uncapping the bottle and drinking the liquid. As promised, the liquid is nothing but water, the cooling liquid making my already cold body much colder. But I continue to drink on until every last drop is done. Then the show begins. My hand clutching the bottle opens as the bottle falls to the ground, shattering. I stagger backwards, falling onto the bed and clutching my throat as I gasp for air. I hear Linnate let out a manic laugh as my body goes limp after my performance of struggling and doing my best to barely breathe so as not to move my body.

"Alister, go in and check to see if this bitch is dead." The sound of the lock being unlocked and the creak of the cell door opening has my heart beating quickly in anticipation. This is a critical moment, and Alister and I have to be in sync for this part to go right. Footsteps approach me before two fingers press against my neck. After some time, the fingers are moved, and a sigh escapes his lips.

"It's done, My Lady, the Prince's Pet is dead," He confirms.

"Good. As promised, you and your daughter are free to go after you clean up here. Make sure no trace is left." With that, the click of heels echoes down the hall with Linnate's departure, and I wait patiently.

"Stay away from me!" I hear a girl scream, and I open my eyes to see Alister walk toward his daughter.

"Alice, it's not what you-"

"You killed a woman, father!" Alice cuts him off. I sigh, sitting up and stretching, deciding to end my acting so that Alister can clear up this misunderstanding.

"Actually, he is helping me to expose Linnate for the vile bitch she is." I state, watching Alice whirl towards me in shock as her father quickly unties her hands and removes the collar around her neck.

"You... You are alive?" She asks, and I nod, walking outside the cell and taking a closer look at the poor girl. Alister finishes checking over his daughter, asking what type of treatment she had faced in Linnate's care, and I wait, allowing the two some time together.

"So you never really killed-" Alice asks her father, and he chuckles, pulling his daughter into a hug.

"No, dear, I could never kill. Besides, Lyra here is pregnant with the Prince's child." I hear a gasp after Alister answers his daughter, smiling encouragingly at the shocked girl, who is only a few years younger than myself, before turning to where Linnate always enters and exits from.

"So, how do we exit this place?" I ask.

"Just follow me, Miss Lyra," Alister answers, taking his daughter's hand and leading us through the hall. We pass many cells, some filled with skeletons that cause my stomach to churn, some empty and filled with dust and mildew. I can see Alice shivering, from cold or fright, I do not know, but I send the girl a reassuring smile as she turns back to look at me, hoping that everything will be okay. We come to the end of the hall soon enough. A wooden door is closed but thankfully not locked as Alister pulls it open, revealing a dark passageway leading into the unknown.

"I can only show you the way out as close to the Palace as possible. Linnate never allowed me to venture further than the exit and entrance." Alister explains, and I nod, motioning for the man to take the lead again. We climb a staircase in the dark, all three of us being careful not to trip or fall, especially myself, to protect my baby. None of us says anything so as not to be caught by anyone. Alice screams when something skitters by our feet, causing me to jump and hold onto the poor girl until the familiar chitter of a mouse is heard, and I chuckle.

"It's just a mouse, hun. They won't hurt you." I reassure, holding the girl until her breathing stabilizes. After reassuring her that she will be okay, the three of us continue our trek until a light at the end of the tunnel appears, and we breathe a sigh of relief. The three of us soon emerge outside, the smell of wildflowers sweeping past us, and I recognize where we are instantly.

"The front of the Palace is that way." Alister points to the right, but I chuckle, turning to the left where the study is, and a flame of hope ignites inside me.

"No, that is too far; I know a shortcut." With that, I start running in the direction of the one room I know only few have access to, seeing the familiar area I first came out of when I was lost in the secret passageways beforehand. It takes what I assume to be another five minutes, and I hear the yips of two familiar dogs, and my eyes tear up.

"Nova, Chaos!" I call out, the yips going silent before the rush of paws in the tall grass can be heard, and my pups surround me. I smile, laughing as I hold my wolfdogs, kneeling on the ground as they lick my cheek.

"Nova and Chaos, get back, you naughty-" A voice calls out, Elisa turning the corner and freezing as soon as she sees me.

"Miss Lyra!" the maid exclaims, rushing to my side and kneeling on the ground beside me, wrapping her arms around me.

"You're okay. You're alive!" My friend sobs. I smile, my own tears falling from my eyes.

"I can explain later, but I need to get to the ceremonial hall. I have to warn Alekai about Linnate." I state to Elisa, instantly getting to my feet only to sway as a rush of dizziness causes me to fall. Arms hold me upright as Alister looks at me with concern in his eyes. Alice joins me on my other side and blocks the pups from jumping on me.

"You need to be careful, Miss Lyra. You are pregnant with the future Heir, after all." Alister warns. I agree, thanking the man for his concern before standing straight, the dizzy feeling fading away. I can see Elisa's questioning look, but I simply smile. Now is not the time for explanations. Elisa seems to understand, coming to replace Alister by my side, and the two help me finish the journey to the study where we promptly enter the room. A shocked Adam stands and rushes to me, pulling me in for a hug.

"Lyra, I am so happy you are okay!" my guard exclaims, his eyes with dark circles surrounding them, taking in my appearance with relief and guilt.

"I should have-"

"Adam, I need to get to Alekai. This reunion can wait; now move." I cut my friend off, pulling away and maneuvering around him to exit the room. I hear Elisa scold him as the group of four people and two wolfdogs follow me down the halls of the Palace, taking multiple turns until we come across a set of large double doors gilded with gold and the royal crest. Guards are standing at attention blocking us from entry.

"Let me in!" I state, standing tall and proud as I try to intimidate these me.

"Sorry, but we are under strict order not to let anyone through." One states, only to have Adam lift him by the collar of his shirt in anger.

"Now, you listen to me. This is Lyra Roselette, the love of our King Alekai's life who has been missing for the last few days. You can and WILL let us through this instance." His threatening demeanour works because the moment this guard is released, his partner and him open the intricate doors just in time.

"Ladies and Gentlemen, I present to you King Alekai Mathews Gabrielle Nightwood." The priest calls out, the room erupting into cheers. The doors slam against the walls, the crowd instantly quieting to see who interrupted the ceremony. I slowly stroll in as another wave of dizziness takes over me, and Elisa rushes to support my body.

` "Lyra!"

Chapter 32

"L-Lyra." Alekai repeats my name in disbelief, slowly walking down the stage before sprinting to my side and instantly pulling me into his arms. Tears roll down my face at the familiar scent of roses and mint washes over me, my own arms wrapping around him. I am finally where I belong, beside Alekai and in his arms.

"Where have you been for the last six days?" Alekai sobs, his body shaking as his own tears fall into my hair. I sob harder, realizing that what I thought was two days held captive was actually longer. Six days spent away from the man I love, six days of him looking for me frantically.

"Li-Linnate. She abducted me." I answer between sobs, feeling Alekai stiffen as he pulls away to look at me, his tear-filled eyes also holding rage in them.

"You sure?" He asks, and I nod, my sobs making it hard to speak.

"Guards!" I hear the sounds of men standing at attention, ready for their King's order.

"Arrest Lady Linnate for treason against the Crown and harming the betrothed of the King, the future Queen of Symphrain." Loud gasps fill the room as guards make their way to the front seats, where Linnate is quickly surrounded by four burly men, instantly captured after a futile attempt at escaping.

"Please gag her so she cannot speak." I call out after calming my sobs enough to speak, watching as Linnate goes to say something only to have a guard stuff some form of fabric into her mouth. I smirk, feeling triumphant as the bitch sends a hate-filled glare my way.

"Your Majesty, you cannot be serious!" A man stands, and I glare at him, Alekai standing protectively between this man and me as he marches towards us.

"Oh, but I am. Lady Lyra was abducted six days ago from our room. Whoever took her left no trace but one thing they missed, a book with a message stating "Save Me" in Lyra's handwriting." Alekai explains, the room exclaiming in shock and asking about the rumour of me leaving in the dead of night only leaving a note behind.

"Lies, of course, a rumour I made while searching for my fiancée." Alekai answers. But the man in front of us is seething with rage, sending a glare toward me.

"I refuse to believe the words of a slave. My daughter is innocent!" This reaction explains a lot, and I chuckle, looking around the ceremonial hall and noting the monitors that display Alekai standing together in front of Linnate's Father.

"You may not believe me, but video proof is all we need." I state, taking the necklace off and motioning for Elisa, who quickly takes the necklace. Before she runs off, I whisper instructions into her ear to skip some of the video, explaining I did not want Linnate's pregnancy to be revealed. Elisa looks at me in shock and then nods before sprinting off toward the stage. The room is filled with soft murmurs, some questioning how I can take off the luxury collar, others talking about how despicable Linnate is. The video of the day I was kidnapped is shown first, my attempt to escape only to be captured and the note I left behind, me being carried by someone out of the room through a hidden passageway and the trek to the catacombs. The video is muffled before it goes blank, only for the images of yesterday and this morning to be played. A loud gasp sounds from the crowd when Alister reveals Linnate's affair with the previous King as well as the fact his daughter was kidnapped by Linnate to force Alister to help her. Her plot was revealed to kill me and my unborn child, the heir of Symphrain, inside me. Elisa looks to Alekai and I, and he signals for her to end the video transmission.

"As you can see, your daughter is vile, and if I am not mistaken, so are you. Guards, take Lord Rushard away as well." Alekai orders, the father-daughter duo being dragged out of the ceremonial hall.

"Alekai, don't harm her. She is pregnant with your half-sibling." I whisper, the dizzy feeling returning but stronger this time. I want to say something else, but my vision blurs, and I feel my body growing weak, happy that Alekai has his arms wrapped around me before my legs give out and darkness consumes me.

∽

"She is indeed pregnant, Kai. Linnate did not lie about that." A quiet voice pulls me from the darkness, and I groan, my eyes feeling weighed down as I try and open them. Two familiar voices converse quietly, the words fading as two sets of footsteps alert me to them walking away. Turning towards their direction, I finally open my eyes to see Alekai, and Doctor Ridley standing by the bedroom doors, deep in conversation.

"Al-Alekai." I call out softly, watching the man I love straighten and turn towards where I lay, a look of relief on his face as he rushes to the bed and plants a kiss on my forehead.

"Thank god you are okay." He sighs out, our foreheads pressed together.

"Where am I?" I ask, taking a look at the dimly lit room as best as I can as Alekai pulls away, his hands taking hold of my left one.

"Hospital wing. You fainted after revealing Linnate's true colours to the Nobles, and I rushed you here. Part of me wanted to make sure that her revealing you are pregnant was real and not a ploy against us." Alekai answers, explaining his intentions of bringing me to Doctor Ridley. I turn and smile at the old Doctor, him coming to stand beside Alekai as he too smiles at me.

"Glad to see you are back, Lyra." He greets me, and I chuckle.

"Glad to be back," I reply.

"We already know the answer, but I must ask out of protocol. Is the baby Alekai's?" I smile, placing my right hand on my flat stomach, Doctor Ridley confirming that I am indeed pregnant and the future of our country is being created inside me.

"Yes. He is the only person I have been with." I answer, a large hand resting on my own, and I turn to see Alekai looking at me, unshed tears in his eyes.

"We are going to be parents!" He exclaims in a whisper, and I nod, turning my hand over under his and linking our fingers together.

"Well, we can still do a paternity test if you two would like. There may be some nay-sayers when the little royal is born." Doctor Ridley suggests. I agree instantly, not wanting trouble to be stirred anymore after the last few days I have experienced and see a shocked expression on Alekai.

"We don't have to, Lyra." He states, and I roll my eyes.

"I know that, but this will shut up those against us. I am doing this for us, for our years to come as King and Queen." I reassure him, seeing a look of relief on his face as he bends forward and places a soft kiss on my lips.

"Hey, kissing and cuddling only. The future Queen has been through hell and needs lots of rest." Doctor Ridley exclaims, causing me to giggle as Alekai rolls his eyes.

"So no sex for a while, I assume, Doc." It's a statement, not a question, as Alekai turns to look at Doctor Ridley, who nods his head.

"Nope. Lyra needs to rest and get proper food in her. These last six days, she has barely eaten by the looks of her bloodwork." Doctor Ridley confirms. My stomach grumbles at the mention of food, and I blush, now realizing how hungry I am. The two men chuckle, Doctor Ridley giving me the okay to go to bed and relax, but I ask if I can go to the coronation ball.

"As long as you sit and relax all night and maybe have one or two slow dances, you may go. If I find out you pushed yourself, I will put you on bed rest, young lady." I accept this recommendation, and so does Alekai as I am scooped into his arms and carried away from the hospital wing. We take the regular route through the Palace halls to our quarters, passing by the coronation guests and Palace workers who bow or curtsy in our direction. The attention makes me blush, and I hide shyly in Alekai's chest.

Once in the safety of our bedroom, I notice it has been renovated, including a few security cameras in the common area and facing the secret passageway doors. Alekai carries me straight to the bathroom, where a bath filled with vanilla-scented bubble bath greets us along with a cart filled with food. The sight causes my stomach to growl loudly. Alekai sets me on the edge of the bathtub, helping me to undress. I remind him to take the note out of my pocket and put it somewhere safe before he helps lower me into the water, before removing his own clothes and joining me. The warmth from the water seeps into my sore muscles, and I relax against his chest, with Alekai feeding me food from the cart.

"I am sorry, Lyra." He whispers, his chin resting on my shoulder after helping me bathe and deciding to soak a little longer before we have to attend the ball.

"For what?" I asked, confused at this sudden apology.

"I couldn't protect you properly, and you almost died twice now by the Rushard family."

"You couldn't have known they would try to kill me." I reassure him, turning around to straddle his lap and forcing Alekai to look at me.

"But you are so important to me. I have watched you for years and knew just how much I loved you." He blurts out, only to cover his mouth with wide eyes. I stare at Alekai in shock, wanting to put some distance between the two of us until his free arm wraps around me, keeping me in place.

"I can explain!" He backtracks, and I cross my arms over my chest.

"You better." He takes a deep breath, closing his eyes as I wait patiently for this explanation. I don't wait long as he opens his eyes to stare out the window.

"When I was younger, I used to sneak out of the Palace. Even back then, Joseph wasn't a good father and would rather be with some random maid over teaching me how to rule. Elisa and I would change into regular clothes and take the passageways out the Palace and towards the city." He begins, and I nod. I remember the few times news would spread that the Crown Prince was missing, many buildings on lockdown as a child until he was found.

"Well, one day, I went to the poverty-stricken part of the city. The only well-maintained building was a church. There they had choir practice, and this one girl always stood out. I remember going every week to sit in the pews and listen, sometimes bringing novels to read, sometimes bringing work. I did this for three years until one day she stands behind me, asking me what I am doing and scaring me so badly I thought I had a heart attack." He chuckles, and a memory surfaces from four years ago. It was my last year of choir as school was picking up, and for years I watched a handsome teen around my age come into the church, always listening. I was shy and scared to approach him, but becoming friends with Jaida and Aime brought me out of my shell. So I took a leap of faith after practice and went up to the boy.

"What you up to?" I asked the boy, watching him jump in fright and fall onto the stone floor. Without meaning to, I started giggling; the way he fell sprawled out was a funny sight for a fourteen-year-old.

"N... Nothing." The boy replied with a blush across his face and emerald eyes holding an emotion I couldn't see.

"Well, it sure looks like something." I retorted, walking around and picking up the scattered pages. The boy gets to his feet, thanking me as I hand over the papers. I sat down at the pew he previously occupied.

"I've seen you come in for the last three years. Sometimes with another girl, sometimes on your own. Are you planning to join the choir?" I pointed out, asking the question I had always wanted to ask.

"No, I can't sing. But I like coming to listen to you sing. You sing like an angel." I blushed at his compliment, turning to look out the window as I played with my hair.

"I don't want to be an angel. Angels are bound by laws and trapped," I stated, hoping my dress covered the bruise on my leg from the kick Father gave me yesterday.

"Well then, what do you want to be?" the boy asked, and I smiled. Then, out the window, I saw white doves fly past and into the vast sky.

"I want to be a bird so I can be free," I admitted, getting a chuckle in response.

"Okay, Little Songbird, I will never call you an angel again." I smiled, turning to look at the boy, his emerald-green eyes watching me, causing my cheeks to heat up. Then, the church bells rang, and I froze, quickly standing and ready to rush out the door for curfew, only for someone to grab my wrist gently, stopping me in my tracks.

"What's your name, Songbird?" The boy asked, and I smiled.

"Lyra. What's yours?"

"Kaito." I smiled at the boy and released my wrist from his hand, letting him know that I had to go and hoped to see him again soon.

"I never saw you after that. Honestly, it was a fluke that day, walking into the Pet store and finding you. I never thought of owning a slave, but seeing those men staring at you pissed me off." He sighs, rubbing a hand over his face in frustration as the realization that the boy who was my first crush is the man I love today.

"And then I went and acted like them instead. I felt terrible, but for once, I had the one thing I wanted, the one I knew I could never have if my father had a say in it. And I hurt you." He continues, and I smile sadly, wrapping my arms around his neck and holding him close.

"I already forgave you for that night, Kai, because I love you," I whisper reassuringly, feeling his lips kiss my shoulder as he holds me close.

"I know I said you were my fiancée in the ceremonial hall, but that was–"

"To protect me, I know. So why don't you ask me?" I finish his sentence, a playful smirk on my face, when Alekai pulls away to look at me in shock.

"What?!"

"I am not going to repeat myself, Kai." I roll my eyes, chuckling at his reaction before a pair of lips crash into mine in a heated kiss, which lasts only a few seconds before ending a little too quickly for my liking.

"Lyra, will you marry me and be my Queen, my life partner and soulmate?" He asks, eyes staring into my soul, and I smile.

"Yes."

Chapter 33

I stare at myself in the mirror, the white fit-and-flare ball gown unable to conceal my two-month baby bump as Elisa helps style my hair into simple curls and Arabess orders maids about. Soon, I will go from Lyra Roselette to Lyra Nightwood, Queen of Symphrain. To think about four months ago, I was sitting in a cage on display, ready to be sold, only to end up in love, pregnant, and soon to be Queen of my country.

"It's almost time," Arabess calls out excitedly, coming to stand beside me, her royal blue gown stunning on her.

"I am a little nervous. What if I am not a good Queen?" I blurt out, my fingers playing with the white gold diamond engagement ring Alekai placed on my finger, something to show we were each other's while at the Coronation Ball. As ordered by Doctor Ridley, I remained seated, with Arabess making sure I was on the throne meant for the Queen while she sat on another decorative chair beside me. She kept me company and helped me navigate the multitude of Noble Ladies and Gentlemen who came to congratulate Alekai as King and me as the woman pregnant with the future heir. Since that day, Arabess has been training me in the ways of being a Queen with one condition from Alekai, that we were to be equals in ruling.

"You'll be perfect. You have already helped with so much this past month, including working on a new bill to abolish the slave trade again." Arabess states and I smile, feeling reassured.

"Your Majesty, Lady Lyra, Alekai asked me to present you with a surprise before we make our way to the cathedral. Elisa cuts in, causing the two of us to look at her as she turns to the door.

"Come in!" Curious, I stand from my seat as the door opens, and two familiar ladies I have been worried about walk inside.

"Aime! Jaida!" I call out, tears falling from my face as I lift the front of my gown and rush to the two I call my sisters. They greet me with open arms, the three of us hugging each other as we cry tears of Joy. He did it. Alekai found my friends, my sisters.

"Lyra, you look stunning," Jaida exclaims, her long red locks now a short bob. I look in shock for a moment. The Heiress to the Roland estate and land always loved her long hair that reminded her of her deceased mother and only had the maids trim the ends when needed.

"You look different. I love the hair!" I state, getting a chuckle from my friend.

"It was time to move on and try something new. Lyham showed me that." She replies, and I take a step back.

"Lyham as in-"

"Duke Lyham of the Lyham Blackcreek Estate, yes. He was the one who bought me." Jaid answers, and I give her a look. She just shrugs, and I accept that this is a story for after the wedding.

"At least you had the man you've been in love with for ages, Jaida. I had my enemy." Aime groans, but instead of the usual look of hatred, I see one of love.

"Dorian bought you!" I scream, seeing Aime smile and blush, her pixie-cut aqua hair longer after four months of not seeing each other.

"No, his father bought me as a gift for Dorian. And before you ask, we are engaged, and I will explain later. First, you Lyra have to tell us how you became Queen!" Aime concedes. I go to say something but am cut off by Arabess.

"My daughter-in-law can explain to you ladies later. Right now, we are running a little late, and all three of you need your makeup redone." My mother-in-law states, with two maids waiting behind her as we are ushered back to the dressing table to have our makeup redone. It is then that I realize my chosen sisters are wearing the bridesmaid dresses designed by Aime's father for my wedding, and I smile. I have a man I am in love with, a mother-in-law who adores me, my chosen sisters by my side, and a baby on the way. Life is perfect.

With our make-up fixed, we are ushered into a limousine and driven straight to the cathedral, where Uncle Elyse is waiting to help all three of us ladies out before turning to look at Arabess with a smile.

"Are we still on for our date tomorrow, Ara?" He asks, and she blushes, leaving Aime, Jaida and I looking on in shock.

"How about we focus on Lyra today and talk later." She answers, giving me a hug before rushing into the cathedral, the wedding march beginning to play through the open doors. My friends smile at me, Uncle Elyse giving each of us a hug before Jaida and Aime too enter the cathedral, a bouquet of flowers in each of their hands. Elisa helps me up the steps on my right with Uncle Elyse on my left.

"I am grateful you are letting me give you away." The Duke states, and I smile, resting my head against his shoulder as we wait for our cue.

"You're a father to me, Uncle Elyse. There is no other person I would choose." With that, our signal is made, and Uncle Elyse guides me into the cathedral, past the front entrance and through double doors. A long cream carpet leads to where Alekai waits for me, tears in his eyes. With tear-filled eyes of my own, I walk steadily toward my love. After Uncle Elyse hands me to Alekai, the ceremony is a blur. My thoughts solely focus on the fact that this is my new life, this is my husband, and this is my fairytale ending I always wanted after Mother passed away. My eyes never leave his, not until the traditional "You May Now Kiss the Bride" Is exclaimed and his strong, soft lips descend onto my own. This kiss is one of passion and love, held with a promise that no matter what happens, I will never be alone. I will always have my husband, Alekai, with me and our little family that is growing. With us legally declared husband and wife, The Priest asks me to kneel as he continues to the next part of today's schedule, crowning me Queen. I keep my head bowed, Alekai moving to stand beside his mother as the Priest says the simplest phrase we agreed upon.

"Do you, Lyra Nightwood, vow to be a just Queen and rule alongside your Husband, King Alekai Nightwood?" He asks, and I smile.

"I do." With that, a crown is placed on my head. Alekai comes to help me stand and places a soft kiss on my cheek, his left hand resting on my stomach where our little Prince or Princess grows.

"I love you." He whispers as we walk down the aisle as husband and wife, our destination being the Palace—our home—to celebrate our love for each other with the people who support and love us.

"I love you too, Kai. You and our little Princess." I chuckle, surprising him even more.

"Princess!" He asks, stopping outside the limousine.

"It's a girl."

Epilogue

"Jesus, and I thought I had it bad in the beginning," Aime states, taking a bite of the donuts Ali made for us to enjoy with our tea in the royal garden. It has been a month since returning from our honeymoon, when Alekai and I travelled the country not only to get to know our people and what they need but also to visit historical sites that were once popular when Symphrain was once Canada. Niagara Falls was my favourite spot during the trip.

"You really do have a Cinderella story, as twisted as it is, with coming from poverty and becoming our Queen," Jaida adds, causing me to chuckle.

"I got lucky. I also had a great school life because of you two," I add, smiling as I lean back and relax in my chair.

"That and me making you look super hot for the club that landed you a Prince," Aime points out, and I roll my eyes.

"It also got us kidnapped, sold, raped... Shall I continue?" Jaida points out sarcastically, causing Aime to throw a croissant at the Heiress.

"Thanks, I was craving that," Jaida exclaims, placing her hand on her stomach, a small bump evident as well. I grin, turning to look at Aime, looking at her bump, the next batch of best friends to come.

"Is your mother-in-law adopting that bitch's daughter when she's born?" Jaida asks and I sigh.

"Yes, Linnate is expected to give birth in three months. After that she will be executed." I answer honestly, frowning at the thought of that vile woman living in a guest room guarded twenty-four-seven until Alekai's sister is born. Only those trusted by Alekai, Arabess and I know about the pregnancy, one that will be played off as a miracle baby for Arabess as soon as the child is born. With the Rushard family being stripped of their title and executed for treason, the property seized will go to Princess Millan when she comes of age.

"Well we are just happy knowing that she will be gone for good and can no longer hurt you or your baby." Aime states, placing her hand on my shoulder as she sends me a warm smile, one I reciprocate with my own.

"So, Aime, it's your turn for story time." I state, sipping my tea and changing the subject as Elisa chuckles behind me.

"I guess it is." My friend sighs as we get comfortable, ready for her tale of how fashion chained her to her enemy-turned-fiancé, Dorian.

Acknowledgement

This book has been a little over a year in the making. At first, I wanted to publish I Am Yours on February 14th, 2021, after the success my first to novels had. I had started it November 2020 after unfortunately getting sick with covid-19.

I was so excited to have a book in a genres I am not familiar with [Erotica] be released and had so many plans but unfortunately my family took a loss when my brother Ryan passed from covid-19.

This loss took a toll on me mentally, emotionally and physically. I lost my best friend, my biggest supporter and the man who basically kept me locked up in his room until I stopped procrastinating and get a few chapters done for what ever book I was working on. I felt lost and like there was no hope.

Eventually, I learned a new normal, reached out for help and when January 2022 came barging in I made it a mission for me to finish this novel, a novel my brother wanted to Read when finished, a novel that I started writing sitting in his room as he gammed with his friends on the PS4 while handing me a drink from the mini-fridge.

With the help of my parents, friends and fans of my novels I was able to bring this work to life and know that this is the first step to a future with my guardian angel looking over me, most likely screaming "Finally ALANA!" some where above as I type this note.

So to those going through a rough time like I did, contemplating if ending it all is the right choice or not - Keep fighting. I promise you that right now life may seem hopeless and meaningless, but the people who love you here in the world of the living and watching over you in the afterlife want you to live your life to the fullest.

I want to end with a "Thank You" to my brother Ryan, for being the one to support me when I first started writing in 2015 on Wattpad and for being the one to say, "Fuck It and publish already!", to me when we both lost our jobs to the pandemic.

You may not be here with me now, but one day we will meet again and I can tell you about my life after your passing.

About the Author

Born and raised in Brampton Ontario - also known at "The Flower City"- Alana Dyer started her relationship with books on a "Hate/Hate" relationship as a child that quickly became a passion for reading as she found that novels can bring you places never seen before.

From finding her love of reading, Alana Dyer soon began writing little stories as a child, and in 2015 with the discovery of Wattpad, Alana started writing seriously with the hopes of one day publishing. Five years later after writing for a loyal fanbase, Alana debuted August 30th, 2020, on Amazon with her first full length novel "The Runaway Breeder".

Now in 2023, Alana Dyer has published 6 novels and two Novelettes under the pen name A. Dyer and spends her days writing, playing with her many pets and planning to expand the distributions of her books.

Rejection Series

Three she-wolves learn that life can take a turn for the worst and those who are supposed to love you can become your worst enemies. When the Moon Goddess and fate play a cruel card that shatters each of their hearts and a budding war is on the horizon can each one find their true strength that lie within and figure out just who is the mastermind in the war that will change the fate of the werewolf race?

Follow Amberle and her Full Moon Rejection in "Rejection on the Full Moon"

See if Geminie's soul mate regrets "Rejecting the Future Moon Goddess"

Can "Rejection to the Alpha King's Daughter" bring out the true Werewolf Queen in Crystalline

And will these girls be able to piece together the true Soulless Evil that hides behind his War?

Rejection on the Full Moon
Book 1

Soulless - werewolves who have turned rogue with no humanity left, giving in to their beastly urges.

Rejection - an act in which your soulmate rejects the mate bond, causing immense pain to the rejected.

These are the challenges Amberle Crest must overcome after becoming an outcast amongst the wolves her age due to an event outside of her control.

When her mate rejects her on her eighteenth birthday, Amberle realizes that living in a pack where the majority would rather use her as a slave than treat her as an equal is not worth the pain. She becomes the notorious wolf, Fire Foot, vowing that everyone would regret how they treated her, as she leaves her pack in the past.

Now a ghost forgotten by those that tormented her, Amberle does whatever it takes to survive as a lone wolf. A fateful day changes her lonely life to one full of happiness and hope—until ghosts from her own past call for aid in ridding their pack of the Soulless who threatens all wolf kind.

Faced with new friends, old foes, and the threat of a building army, will Amberle be able to fight the ghosts of her past to cherish the pack she has found or will an old mate claim her before a second chance mate can show her what being treasured by someone is all about?

Rejecting the Future Moon Goddess
Book 2

Soulless - werewolves who have turned rogue with no humanity left, giving in to their beastly urges.

Rejection - an act in which your soulmate rejects the mate bond, causing immense pain to the rejected.

Moon Goddess - the deity that created the werewolf race whom her creation worship

Omega - The lowest ranked wolf in the pack sometimes treated as nothing more than a slave or an object

These are the things Geminie Blake learns after being blamed for the tragic Deaths of her Alpha and Luna. With the pack turned against her and failing to shift as a wolf, Geminie faces challenges every day with the hope of one day gaining freedom or her mate saving her. But when her fated soul mate ends up being her ex-best friend and the son to the late Alpha and Luna rejects her, Geminie's life changes drastically.

Learning that she is not Geminie Blake - daughter to the Beta couple - but Geminie Starlite - daughter to the Moon Goddess and Future Moon Goddess herself - Geminie quickly faces the new challenges thrown her way as she navigates her wolf form and Goddess powers, creating a pack that rivals that of Blood Moon and building her life from scratch to one day take up the mantel as Moon Goddess becomes her priority.

Now, thriving and loving herself for who she is, Geminie forces the past behind her as she waits for her second chance at love. When her first mate requests help and aid from a threat created by Soulless and a potential Leader of the wolves that have lost their Humanity, Geminie is forced to face the wounds left unhealed and return to the place she called hell for eleven years of her life.

Will Geminie be able to overcome the scars left by years of abuse and find love once and for all, or will the panful wounds of her past and threat from the Leader of the army of Soulless ready to kill at a moments notice take the last bit of happiness this young Goddess has left.

Rejection to the Alpha King's Daughter
Book 3

Soulless - werewolves who have turned rogue with no humanity left, giving in to their beastly urges.

Rejection - an act in which your soulmate rejects the mate bond, causing immense pain to the rejected.

Moon Goddess - the deity that created the werewolf race whom her creation worship

Omega - The lowest ranked wolf in the pack sometimes treated as nothing more than a slave or an object

Alpha King/Queen - The rulers of the werewolf nation

Runt - The smallest of the wolf pack, usually ignored or bullied for being the smallest

Crystalline Thorn grows under the abuse by her father as she trains to take the throne one day and become the Alpha Queen, leader of every wolf in the werewolf nation. She dreams of the day when she meets her mate and be accepted as a strong Queen, especially since she is a runt.

But her dream is soon shattered when on the day of an Alliance her mate discovers her "weak" form and rejects her promptly leading to her father disowning her and her hopes to inherit the throne is dashed. But that is the least of her worries. Soon, with the help of Geminie and Amberle, Crystalline learns of a war that has been brewing for thousands of years, of a destiny that has been written in the stars by the original Moon Goddess - Luna - and the Goddess of Destiny - Morai - have placed upon her and her connection to the Lost Princess.

Will Crystalline be able to retrieve her throne?

Will she accept the mate that rejected her or chose the second chance mate?

Or will the weight of responsibility handed to her crush her entirely?

The Run

"The cage doors are released and I open my sapphire coloured eyes, dashing out of the prison and into the forest.

Seven days for the full moon to be blue.

Seven days from the starting line to the finish

Seven days, that's how long I had to make it to the lodge as an unmated female."

Legends of werewolves have gone back centuries. Always including the Moon Goddess and her blessing of soulmates to the beings she created. But the ugly truth is there is no such thing as soulmates. There is only The Run.

An event created centuries ago held twice a year during a blue moon where she-wolves run from their male counter parts. If they are captured, they are mated and marked, claimed by whoever captures them first.

No one is exempted from this event - not even Grace Harvest.

After being able to avoid attending the event since turning eighteen, Grace finds herself unable to find an excuse not to participate this time. With her last hope of remaining unmated until she can fall in love, she makes a bet with her Alpha. If she wins, he can no longer force wolves of his pack to participate in The Run and allow them to find love. If he wins, Grace will be mated, and her pack mates are forced to go no matter what.

But what will happen when she meets a golden haired wolf by the name Caden Wolfrain, who instantly captures her attention. Will she do all she can to win the bet, will Caden win her heart or will the secrets Caden keeps force her to cut ties with this golden haired wolf without a second thought no matter the heart break.

Books by the Author

CONTACT THE AUTHOR

 alana.dyer.author@
hotmail.com

 author.alana.dyer

 alana.dyer

 Alana Dyer
@alana.dyer.author

E-BOOK | PAPERBACK | HARDCOVERS
available where books are sold

Don't miss out!

Visit the website below and you can sign up to receive emails whenever Alana Dyer publishes a new book. There's no charge and no obligation.

https://books2read.com/r/B-A-LXGX-HFPOC

Connecting independent readers to independent writers.

www.ingramcontent.com/pod-product-compliance
Lightning Source LLC
Chambersburg PA
CBHW070934250626
47159CB00009B/3239